For my daughter

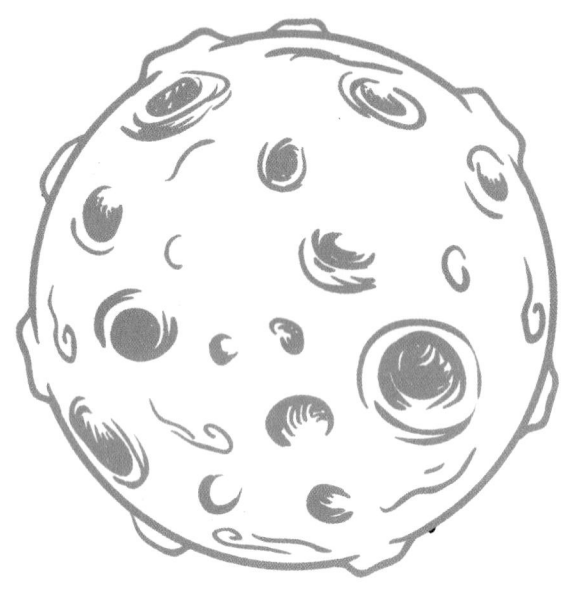

The Moonbeams
and the Mission of Great Importance

WRITTEN BY
AJ SWIRLES

ILLUSTRATED BY
EDUARDO PAJ

Published in association with Bear With Us Productions

©2019 AJ Swirles

The right of AJ Swirles as the author of this work has been asserted by his in accordance

with the Copyright Designs and Patents Act 1988.
All rights reserved, including the right of reproduction

in whole or part in any form.

INTRODUCTION

Have you ever wondered whether ghosts and goblins actually exist? How about Bigfoot, aliens, The Tooth Fairy, and monsters under the bed? Are they real, or are they just figments of the human imagination?

There are many things that remain a mystery to us, and many things left unexplained. What if you were able to peek behind the curtain of reality, and see exactly who is responsible for it all?

If you only knew the truth; the truth that all of our mystery is created for us, by someone with a legion of tiny mischief makers, expert in the art of the mysterious.

They are sent by The Man when The Moon is full, and they are...

The Moonbeams

Boid planted his feet firmly upon the desolate Moon surface, spread his toes in the dust, and took a good look around. It was great to be on top, it always made him feel free. After a long month in the Moonbeam caves on the far side of The Moon, time on the side that faces The Earth was a really nice interlude. As a matter of fact, it happened to be one of his favourite experiences.

He gazed up for a moment, to drink in the breath-taking beauty of the big, blue marble, floating in the darkness above him. It was a familiar canvas to him, but due to its relentless spinning, the portrait was different every time. Today it looked particularly spectacular. The Sun was already rising from behind it, casting streaks of light from its top, like a crown of glittering thorns.

He started a mental countdown. When The Sun rose fully, their position would be bathed in a curtain of light and, when it hit them, he and his team would surf the reflected beams straight to Earth. For approximately one-point-three seconds the rays from The Sun would be their transport, and they would be hurtling at light speed towards the ground with no control over the in-flight entertainment.

Since being just two-inch tall, and only a Youngbeam, Boid had loved all things mysterious. When he heard the stories of the many wild and epic adventures on The Big Blue, he knew he just had to go. So he put in the work at The Earthonaut Academy, and fast became the youngest Earthonaut in Moonbeam history. This made his parents incredibly proud and, when he saw them, they were always glowing with anticipation of stories from his Earth adventures.

But better than that, the missions to Earth were often a real riot, and he got the chance to do cool stuff. Like the time his team carved a giant fallen log into the shape of a serpent monster, and paddled it across Loch Ness. The log was seen by some humans from a distance, who sent a photograph to the newspapers, which then fuelled the legend of The Loch Ness Monster. It was a real hoot, and his claim to fame. He always enjoyed remembering that one. Such a simple thing, but it had earned him near-legendary status amongst his peers. It helped get him promoted to Commander, and now he was orchestrating more of history's greatest illusions, using teams of conjurors, dream-weavers, and mentalists, all highly trained in the mystic arts. He felt immensely proud to be an Earthonaut Commander. Proud to be a six-inch tall Moonbeam master of mystery, and knower of great truths.

His right-hand man, and good friend Jipp made an entrance from beyond the darkness, with his ridiculous large-footed walk; a comical, lolloping stride of which Boid always found amusing. His feet were so long he would have to kick way out in front of him, making it look like his legs had a mind of their own. It tickled him every time he saw it. Jipp was heading towards him, kicking up a dust storm, with legs whirling around, like an octopus trying to swat a fly on a beach. As he approached, Boid laughed internally so as not to offend his friend.

"Here we go again," said Jipp, "The old band back together."

Jipp always said that, before every mission. The joke had long since worn off, but Boid didn't have the heart to tell him that he thought,

It wasn't really such a great catchphrase to have, as an opening line.

"Hey buddy, glad you could join us," Boid replied deeply, stifling a giggle.

Jipp finished his preposterous walking, stopped proudly in front of his comrade, and waited silently, to allow the wake of his dust shadow to disintegrate around him. His wild, sandy hair swooshed and fell into place, whilst his steely gaze betrayed a glint of excitement. Standing there in his cape, he cut rather a swashbuckling figure. He looked a bit like a bearded elf with hilarious feet, but he had confidence, and that counted for a lot. He was also one of Earthonaut Academy's top athletes, and super reliable, which made him extremely useful to have around in a scrape.

"Still something, huh?" Jipp said, looking up at The Earth.

It was something. A big blue something that, with each passing second, looked more and more like it was going to pour a cascade of screeching sunlight from out the top of its head.

"Sure is," Boid replied, as he stood gazing up, anticipation rising within him.

Then, the points of his ears twitched at the sound of giggles from a distance. When he turned to look he saw, bouncing playfully across the plains, two young Earthonauts energised with laughter and excitement. Watching them, it immediately reminded him how he felt his first time on top. When The Earth first revealed its majesty to him it gave him a gut-crippling case of the giggles. He'd since seen cadets almost coming apart at the seams with hilarity on their first mission, and concluded that it was a natural reaction to being shown such a humbling site.

Jipp looked at Boid with sideways eyes, and said, "Rookies?"

"They were chosen by The Man," his friend replied.

Jipp's left eyebrow took a sharp turn north, and he looked clearly surprised. Boid knew his friend thought The Man was getting a bit crazy. He often said,

'He's losing his marbles, that guy. Some of his missions are totally ridiculous.'

The Man was Head of Mission Control, and he was the one who decided who went where, and why. He was revered and feared for his wisdom, gained during a career spanning at least two centuries. He was next level mysterious, seemed to know everything, and ran operations secreted within a secret cave on the far side of the dark side of The Moon. No one had knowledge of what he did in there, because only the sworn few were ever granted access, and he mainly communicated his instructions through written messages delivered by his sour-faced, tight-lipped security detail. He'd been out of sight for so long everyone had long forgotten what he even looked like.

Boid, however, didn't mind not knowing what he looked like because he appreciated the theatre. And besides, he had already received his instructions from The Man.

This mission was one of great importance.

"It's one of the most important missions an Earthonaut can ever partake in," The Man had bellowed, appearing by surprise in the cave before him, as a smoky, hooded apparition.

Boid knew it wasn't really him in person, it was a projection of some kind. But it was a cool trick, so he had made a mental note to try and find out how it was done.

"You see, we have teams that do werewolves, poltergeists, goblins, and trolls," The Man had said, "We have teams that do extraordinary light shows, that make it look like sky beings are visiting The Earth. Some even get to spend a lot of their time dressed as fairies, sitting at the bottom of someone's garden, waiting for attention,"

Boid flinched at the thought of The Fairy Detail. It was a mission he had always tried to avoid. He could see himself in lots of different missions, but could never see himself pulling off looking like a fairy. Not with his barrel chest and mohawk haircut.

"Some still line up on beaches, to create the tides!" The Man had cried incredulously, "Why they still want to do that, I do not know? But I allow them to do it. It seems to keep them happy,"

Boid had always wondered where the idea came from, that

the Moonbeams were solely responsible for creating The Earth's ocean tides. Maybe they had once heard it was The Moon's gravity pulling the water towards it and, over time, it had become lost in translation. Whatever happened, it had become (sort of) tradition to travel to Earth, line up with large boards held out in front, and then charge as one into the waves, to show the ocean who's boss.

"But you, Boid..." he continued, "...You were part of my genius Bigfoot campaign, do you remember that?"

Boid did remember that. It was the time he and sixty-two other Moonbeams, stacked themselves on top of each other's shoulders and webbed their arms together, to form an intricate human-shaped shell. Then they wrapped themselves in an exquisitely crafted human-sized furry Bigfoot costume and, in clumsy unison, stumbled around a snow-capped forest in the moonlight. They spent all night in the woods in the hope of being seen by astonished wilderness explorers, who'd then go home, and tell rip-roaring stories of the time they survived an encounter with the great mythical beast. The end result being the story of Bigfoot being kept alive, with the bonus that the mission would be held within academy legend forever.

However, they couldn't stop laughing, and could barely stand themselves up in character for any good length of time. They regularly fell over, and collapse in hysterical fits at the absurdity of it all, only to get up and try it all over again. It was riotous fun, and especially funny when someone in the middle of the Bigfoot formation said, "Oh no, I think a bit of wee came out," to the groans of those below.

"You owe me one, after that debacle," The Man had said.

"Erm..." Boid had stuttered.

"I want you to remember that this mission is a symbol of the human imagination," The Man continued, "You're kick-starting the beginning of a beautiful journey into the unknown. Call it a little nudge towards discovery."

The smoky apparition, now glistening a faint blue, whistled around him a few times, like a floating snake, and then reformed again before him. This time as a large, scary face with deep red glowing eyes.

"I like to think we've moved on from simple parlour tricks," the big scary face said.

Boid had considered that a bit ironic at the time, given that he was looking directly at one of The Man's 'parlour tricks.'

"We have a more serious obligation. A guardianship, if you will. You see, the humans need their mystery. It fires their minds to enquire and learn, to build and invent, it's their defining characteristic. I like to keep reminding them that they don't know everything, and that there's always something better to reach for. That if they put their minds to it, they can do anything…" he paused for a moment then said,

"You don't think they got to where they are, all by themselves, do you?"

At the time Boid wanted to answer 'Probably', as he happened to agree with Jipp on this one. Some of his missions had started to look a bit strange, and The Man was probably overplaying his own importance, but every time he talked to The Man he could never shake the feeling that he knew something that no one else did.

"Surely, I would be better served doing exactly what I'm doing?" Boid had asked.

"Yes. And what you'll be doing is this mission. For me," The Man had declared,

"Think of it as dropping pebbles in a pond. Each one dropped causes it's own ripples in time. Then, all you have to do is sit back and watch the ripples. Play the long game."

Boid had felt lost at this point, but remembered thinking,

There's no point arguing with him. Do this, and then ask for promotion.

Perhaps then he could join The Freelancers; Earthonauts who chose their own Earthly destinations, free from The Man's oversight. They were The Man's elites, and being one of them would make his parents even prouder. He allowed himself the thought of telling his mother that he would be able to take her to her dream destination, Fiji.

She'd love it in Fiji, he had thought.

"You know what I think when I see rookies, don't you?" Jipp remarked.

"Yes, I do," replied Boid, knowing Jipp was dismissive of all Earthonaut cadets, always calling them 'rookies'. He also knew that Jipp had probably already guessed what sort of mission this was.

"It's one of The Man's bonkers missions, isn't it?" Jipp huffed.

Boid moved closer, and said, "Stick with me, my friend, and we'll be Freelancers before you know it," hoping it would give Jipp hope.

Boid didn't wait for Jipp's reaction, he just looked forward. He could tell his friend wanted to say more, but the cadets were now striding their last few steps in respectful silence, so Jipp didn't say anything. The cadets came to a halt, stood stiffly, and looked up at their Commander with wide-eyed expectation.

Boid's visual assessment was an instant one, and part of his training;

The cadet on the left was tall and gangly, with thick, spiky mulberry hair that seemed to reach for the sky, like a thirsty cactus in a thunderstorm. He had two huge, carrot-gnashing front teeth, that you could probably use to prize open an oil drum in an emergency. His name was Fluff; it was mentioned in the files he'd been given.

From the cadet on the right, he immediately sensed an adventurous spirit. He knew her name to be Luna, and her smile beamed from pointy ear to pointy ear. Her ruby red mane was dutifully tied at the back, but leaving just enough hair free to allow it to wisp unchallenged, around the frame of her cherubic face. She was small with little legs, and he instantly thought she would be good in a nooks and crannies situation. Both cadets were suitably attired in regulation crab-proof armour.

He broke the silence, skipped the introductions, and got straight to the point,

"You are about to experience something you've never

experienced before," he declared,

"Once the light hits, you may feel like your insides are on the outside, and that you're trying very hard not to eat your own face. Some have reported it to feel like time doesn't exist, and that they're experiencing themselves subjectively, free from corporeal form,"

He enjoyed the possibility the cadets didn't know this meant that it would feel as if they were leaving their own bodies, and he secretly rejoiced in knowing big words that others didn't. It was his guilty pleasure.

"Some even say that…" he leant forwards, "…they are at one with the light,"

Then he stood back, crossed him arms, and said, "Personally, I mainly just try to hold down my lunch, and try not to fart."

He himself had never been fond of the light jump, what with all the stretching and twisting of his precious molecules. It was his least favourite part of the mission.

Then, looking them both in the eyes, he quipped,

"I hope your last meal was a tasty one."

Fluff looked up and licked his lips, as if he was remembering a nice tasty pie he had recently eaten, whereas Luna just kept beaming her adorable smile. Boid began to pace seriously, from side to side.

"Now," he continued, "When we land, we always touchdown on a beach and, on the first jump, fifty percent of cadets land face down in the sand,"

He turned his head to glance over to Jipp. His money was on the little one, and the return look from Jipp suggested he thought the same.

"When all of your molecules are put back together it's common to feel a bit…well, weird. On my first time, it felt like my eyes were inside out, my bum cheeks and my real cheeks had swapped places, and my ears were slices of bread. But the effect soon wears off, don't worry,"

The cadets glanced at each other as if they were trying not to laugh.

Boid continued, but his tone had suddenly darkened,

"Now, have you ever been told the story of The Great Bali Beach Crab-off?"

The cadets' faces simultaneously took on a sharp look of concern. He knew they had heard that story, everyone had. It was the mission where a legion of tide-turning Earthonauts were ambushed by a huge, pincer-snapping crab army, as soon as they landed. It was stuff of legend. Pacing ever slower, Boid switched into full story-telling mode, and told the story anyway,

"It happened on a beach in Bali," he said, "One starry night, a whole eighty-eight-strong squadron of tide turning Earthonauts descended into, what my buddy once described as, a living hell,"

He stopped, looked up, and remembered his comrade's traumatised face, as he told of that fateful night,

"The landing was textbook," he said, "They'd gotten into formation and, with tide-turning boards in hand, were about to march into the ocean. When suddenly, from the sand beneath their feet, arose those chilling stalky eyes and huge, razor-sharp claws, snipping and-a snapping,"

Boid held out his hands and tapped his fingertips with his thumbs, to mimic the snips,

"The slowest to react were the heaviest injured, the quickest used their boards for defence, whereas the brightest ones just beamed right on outta there,"

He looked the cadets up and down, gauging their wide-eyed reactions, and continued,

"Now, we never carry weapons. We are sworn to protect all life, not destroy it. But it is now compulsory for all first-timers to be custom-fitted with your own light-weight crab-proof armour,"

The cadets' eyes were momentarily drawn downwards to look at themselves.

"Are you fitted well, cadets?" barked Boid.

"Sir, yes sir!" They cried together,

"Good," replied their Commander, "Because, since its introduction, reports of crab trauma have halved, so think of it as fifty-percent protection. It doesn't mean it's not dangerous, it just means that it's fifty-percent less dangerous. So, if you have anything to say, now is the time."

The two cadets looked at each other as if they were trying to decide who was going to ask the question they had talked about earlier.

"What's our mission, Commander?" Luna took it upon herself to ask that question.

"Strictly on a need to know basis, and I'll let you know when you need to know," came Boid's business-like reply, "Besides, if I told you now, where would the mystery be?"

He was being deliberately cryptic, and because it was so cryptic the cadets nodded their heads in unison, as if to agree that that was a good point. It was more fun for a Moonbeam not to know. At least for now.

"All I can say is..." he said, "...it's a mission of great importance."

Once again, he saw the cadets exchange looks, and could feel their anticipation rising. Luna's broad smile got broader, and Fluff's eyes seemed to do a little dance in his head.

"One last thing," Boid sternly added, "And this is most important. You must remember we have no idea how many light jumps your bodies will allow you. Some Earthonauts can do only a few, whereas some have been doing it for centuries. No one knows why, it's just the way it is. So, if you want a long career, and complete lots of missions, the best thing to do is to keep your Earth time to an absolute minimum."

Boid paused for a moment, and then leant forwards, as if he was sharing a secret,

"This is why I like to return home the very same evening, while The Moon is still in sight. Failure to do so could mean having to wait for the next Full Moon, and potentially leave us without the ability to beam back. Ever. The last thing you want is to end up like those poor Earthtimers down there, wandering, alone, purposeless, stranded,"

He knew they knew the story of The Earthtimers. The one about a small group of Earthonauts that were lost to the vastness of Earth. Unable to return through a light jump, forever doomed to loneliness in the shadows, unable to reveal themselves, for threat of being captured. No one had ever heard from them again.

"This means we're always on the clock, and why I like to be as fast as moonbeamly possible. In, out, job done. So, you'll need to keep up. Got it?"

Boid was willing to allow a few moments for that reality to sink in, but the cadets nodded in urgent compliance, seemingly glaring at something behind him. He turned around to see The Sun had arisen, and the starlight was now crackling across the grey plains of The Moon, like a white wall of lightning. The sight of it made his skin prickle.

Jipp shot Boid a look, and said, "Are you ready to be at one with the light?"

Boid rolled his eyes back at him, and replied,

"Not really. It's one-point-three seconds of pure weirdness."

"What pie did you eat?" asked Jipp.

"Nimbleberry. You?"

"Nimbleberry."

"Good choice," replied Boid, knowing that at light speed most other pies somehow tasted like damp sawdust, dipped in electric gravy.

Boid and Jipp jumped to either side of the mesmerised cadets, and stood in a line to face the oncoming starlight.

Boid yelled, "Assume positions!"

All at once, they dropped to one knee, dipped their heads, and squeezed their eyes tightly shut. There was a crippling shock of whiteness, and their bodies were atomised in an instant. They began to contort and squish, inside and outside, doing a spiral dance through time and space. Boid tried to concentrate on hurtling at light speed towards the big blue ball in front of him. He tried not to notice his body felt like electrified vapour, stretched two-hundred-and-fifty-thousand miles long, or that he had a rising taste of nimbleberry pie, at the back of wherever his throat was.

CHAPTER TWO:
SWORN ENEMIES?

Boid was looking back at himself, from outside of his own body. There was a sharp crack of light, his eyeballs plopped back into his head, and his molecules ended up where they were supposed to be. He looked immediately to his side, to check that his team were okay. They were all down on one knee as before, except for Luna who was face down in the sand. He smiled to himself, glanced knowingly at Jipp, and held out a hand to help her to her feet.

"You'll get the hang of it, cadet," he quietly reassured.

Luna looked a little embarrassed at being one of the fifty-percent face-planters, but was quickly brushing away the sand from her face, and out of her hair. Fluff and Jipp were also getting to their feet, and starting to look around them.

It was a small beach with a modest wooden marina at one end. Around it were several tethered fishing boats slowly bobbing on a tide, lit only by the reflection of The Moon. Boid appreciated the serene picture for a moment. As he did, he felt the faint taste of pie on his tongue being replaced by a strong smell of rotting seaweed, in his nostrils. When he scanned the shore, he could barely see through the darkness. He knew it was important they made their way inland as quickly as possible.

"Okay guys, the plan is to get inland, pronto," he said, "The softer sand is when we're most to vulnerable, so we're going to have to work hard. It's not that easy to walk on, so stay close, and follow me in diamond formation,"

They moved to get in position; Boid in front, Jipp and Fluff to each side, with Luna at the rear. Everyone had a direction to keep an eye on.

Spreading his toes again, and striding on, Boid directed them inland. In the distance he could make out a wave of treetops swaying in the borrowed moonlight, and headed for that. He knew this was a critical moment, and one in which he needed to remain calm and controlled. He didn't feel particularly calm, but he had the ability to never look panicked, everyone commented on it. In The Academy, Jipp would often tell him it was because his face 'just stays in the same permanent grump' and, as he got braver, he would tell him he looked like a 'sulking bulldog'. Boid didn't feel like a sulking bulldog, but he knew he probably looked like one.

As they shuffled silently on, Boid could tell the team were staying as close as they could. Jipp was watching the right, glaring intently into the night. He took a glance back to find Fluff scanning the left, with a rising tension in his eyes. Luna's little legs were pumping hard to keep up at the back, and her head was swivelling back and forth, keeping watch on their back. Good team. So far so good. Focusing ahead, he could now just about make out the beach end, and it appeared to turn from sand to rocks. Land was close by, and the danger would soon be behind them.

Suddenly, from somewhere in front of them, came a clicking sound. It seemed to echo from the thick darkness. Boid felt the tiny hairs on the back of his neck stand up, and his throat instantly lost moisture. The team instinctively stopped in their tracks, and froze.

"Wait," Boid whispered dryly, and he held out his arms protectively.

There was a deathly silence, and they closed their backs in together, to face all directions. Then the clicking started again, louder, and louder, and coming from all around them. It turned to a slow rhythm,

Click-click...snip-snip-snip...click-click...snip-snip-snip.

"Please, don't let that be what I think it is?" Fluff shivered.

Boid noticed the look of fear on the faces of his team, and tried to hide his own rising apprehension. Should they make a break for it, and run as fast as they could? No. He had no idea which direction they would run, or even if they could effectively escape in the undulating sand. He decided to keep everyone still, and see what developed.

Then, from the gloom around them, like sideways-walking spooks in the night, came a cast of crabs, holding aloft their giant, razor-sharp pincers. They looked twice their size, and terrifying. They had eyes on long stalks sprouting from their mottled, pink bodies, that were looking at them, as if they were food. And there were lots of them. Lots of hungry looking eyes.

Boid knew the only way out of this was to use the ancient

Moonbeam ability to communicate with all of Earth's creatures, and try to talk his way out of it. No one had ever explained to him the origin of this ability, but some believed it was because the Moonbeams shared some kind of common ancestry with all of life on Earth. Others believed it was because Moonkind was special in a way that cannot be defined. After much thought Boid had decided that it was because Moonbeams were mystical beings, that did mystical stuff, and that was that.

"Bit far from home ain't you?" came a voice from the largest crab right in front of them.

Boid didn't know if crabs could smile, and it was hard to decide if he was friendly or not, but the crab was asking a question, not snapping them in half, and that was an encouraging start. The voice sounded gravelly, as if he had a tonne of sand in his throat, and Boid immediately thought he might be the boss.

Before anyone could reply a second crab shrugged forward aggressively, and said, "You're trespassing, don't ya know? You're trespassers."

Standing wide, Boid replied, "We come in peace. We're on a mission of great importance."

The crabs let out a soft ripple of laughter, and their eyes started rolling around on their creepy stalks. Something was funny, but Boid wasn't sure what it was. After a few seconds of laughter, the first crab stopped laughing, and the others soon followed. He was definitely the boss.

"You guys have starting saying that a lot," Boss Crab said, mockingly.

Boid wasn't sure what he meant, but he knew his orders. This mission was one of great importance, The Man said so. He just didn't say why.

Suddenly, a third crab made a movement forward with his claw, snipped it menacingly, and said, "I say we snip 'em, boss."

The Earthonauts took in a collective breath, moved back in amongst themselves, and Boid's heart skipped a beat.

"We're not afraid of you!" blurted Luna, bravely.

Boid took a sideways glance at her, and thought about

telling her to keep quiet. Then the laughter started again, but this time just from Boss Crab. As he laughed, his eyes were trained on Luna.

The third crab shuffled sideways towards her and warned, with a slow snip of the pincer, "You should be afraid, Youngbeam, you should be."

Some of the crabs around them joined in with the slow snipping, till it reached that eerie rhythm once more.

Boss Crab lifted up and, with claws held wide, he said, "Okay boys, take it easy."

The crabs laid their bellies to the sand, and the slow snipping stopped.

Boss Crab stopped still, and focused his bulging, stalky eyes at Boid.

"We just want to get off your beach, and get on with our peaceful mission," Boid explained.

"Sure, I get it," Boss Crab barked, "You just wanna get off our beach? You just wanna stomp all over our patch, and be merrily on your way, don't ya?" looking around him, "You wanna trample all over our surf-turf, disturbing our nurseries, sometimes on crucial hatching nights of the year, with no thought of the damage to our young? Is that what you wanna do?"

Boss Crab looked so angry it made Boid feel shrunken, as if the weight of someone else's guilt had just been poured all over him.

"Of course not, no," Boid replied, "I would never ever even think to..."

"You see, that's just it, you don't think. You never do," Boss Crab interrupted, "You all just go about your own mad business, trying to push oceans of water about with your ridiculous boards, with no comprehension of the after effects."

He paused for a moment, and then said, "You do know that it's The Moon's gravity that causes the tides, don't you? I mean… everyone knows that," Boss Crab waved a dismissive claw, and the other crabs grumbled in agreement.

Boid took a step forwards, opened his arms, and said, "Look, this is all news to us..."

"News? News? Everything's news to you lot," interrupted Boss Crab again.

"No, I know about the gravity," pleaded Boid, "That's obvious. To most of us. Well, to some of us. Well, to me it is. But I swear, Moonbeams are sworn to protect all life. We knew nothing of your nurseries."

There was a silence as Boss Crab gazed away, and his menace appeared to soften. Boid immediately saw this as an opportunity to negotiate, so he walked towards him and said,

"How about, after my mission, I make it my number one priority to make sure we steer clear of all nursing beaches in future?"

Boss Crab stopped still, and seemed to raise an imaginary eyebrow.

"Go on..." he said,

Getting closer, with hands cupped around his mouth, Boid whispered,

"We reach a little agreement. I use my influence to keep your young safe in the future, and you use your influence to give us safe passage inland."

"I do have influence, I have lots of influence," Boss Crab muttered to himself, looking away. Then he turned to Boid, and said, "Do you?"

"Yes, I do," Boid replied confidently, "I get to finish my mission, and you become legend with many grateful mother crabs, who no longer need worry about the fall of Moonbeam feet."

Boss Crab raised a claw and seemed to scratch his head, then crouched, pointed his eyes down, and said quietly,

"Listen, some of my guys want nothing more than to snip you all into tiny digestible pieces. Some of them even lost some hatchlings somewhere along the lines. Well, probably...who knows? It's hard to tell these days. Point is they want payback."

Boss Crab's eyes glanced off into the distance for a moment as if he was seeing something in the darkness. Boid followed his look, but could see only black. Then he noticed Boss Crab's claw slowly reach towards him, pincer gaping. His pulse quickened for a moment, but the pincer wrapped around to pull him closer, into a friendly-ish hug.

"But I tell ya what," Boss Crab continued, "I'm gonna take your deal. It ain't a bad deal. I quite like it. I always do good deals. I'm known for it, I tell ya," he smiled knowingly.

Boid nodded his head in compliant agreement, but decided not to shake his hand on it.

"What's your name, soldier?" Boss Crab asked.

"The name's Boid, and I'm not a soldier, I'm an Earthonaut."

"Well, Earthonaut Boid," Boss Crab chuckled, "I kinda like ya. You got moxie, and I like that. But, even though you seem different, and brighter than the rest, don't think I won't hesitate to feed you to my boys if you don't fulfil your obligations," he held his claw to his jaw, mafia style.

"You have my word," Boid swore.

"Okay, my friend, I'll take it. You have safe passage. Go…go on your 'mission of great importance.'"

He lifted himself up, and snipped twice with his left claw. The crabs began to shuffle sideways and, with a slight grumble from some of them, they opened a clear path up the beach. Boid looked at his team, and gestured a flat palm for them to go ahead.

"Thank you," said Boid, with a bow of the head.

"One last thing," Boss Crab said, "You got a little firecracker there," pointing at Luna, "She's got moxie too,"

Boid smiled, because he knew he was right. He had seen her fearlessness when she yelled at the crabs, and had already thought she was going to be an asset. He could tell.

"I noticed," he replied, and nodded in appreciation.

Striding forward, he urged them on to make their way inland with haste, sinister crab eyes piercing the darkness, watching silently, from either side. They made solid progress at first but, at such a pace, Luna's little legs started to look a little heavy in the soft, undulating sand. Then there was the sharp snip of Boss Crab's claws from behind them, and a second later the sand before them started to shake and shudder. Boid was taken by surprise by the mini-earthquake, and instinctively stood still. He held his legs wide, to plant his feet solidly in the sand.

Had Boss Crab changed his mind? he thought, *Was he just toying with us?*

From the depths before them, mysterious grey rock circles vibrated suddenly to the surface and, after a few seconds, there was a perfect path of rocks, leading up to take them clear of the beach. It would make walking across the sand so much easier, and was a good trick, a very good trick. Boid could appreciate a good trick.

"A little something for the Firecracker!" came Boss Crab's gravelly cry.

Luna looked up at Boid, wonder glinting in her eyes, and gave him a huge smile.

"After you, cadet," he said, and gestured her on with a courteous hand.

Without hesitation, she took a leap onto the first rock, and then bounded swiftly to the next, with apparent ease, higher in the air than before. Boid felt the need to allow the others to go first and they did so, immediately following on. Then, holding up the rear, Boid took the leap. As his feet hit the first rock he seemed to spring higher than expected, and it only took the second jump for him to realise that the rocks were not rocks after all. They were stepping on the backs of more crabs, bobbing up and down, all timing it perfectly, to give them an extra boost in their bounce.

As he leapt, he felt a satisfied smile creep over his face. He could hear Luna ahead, giggling uncontrollably as she sprung into the air, propelled by the backs of Earth's most cooperative crabs.

Later, when Boss Crab got back to his hide, it was full of fresh, delicious molluscs for him to eat, which seemed rather mysterious to everyone except him. He had indeed struck a deal. Just not with Boid.

CHAPTER THREE:
THE WONDER/ DANGER OF IT ALL

"Wow, that was amazing!" shrieked Luna as her feet hit the ground.

Boid watched closely as they touched down, one after the other, onto a gravel pathway that ran up the length of the beach. As he joined them, he gave Luna a casual smile, and she grinned back at him in delight. He knew she was enjoying the relief of survival, and felt the same way. He was also pleased because he knew, when he got home, he would be applauded for brokering a peace treaty with their (not so) sworn enemies, The Crabs. It would be seen as a major achievement, make him very popular, and might even help when he asked for promotion. But he had to remain focused, because he had The Man's mission yet to complete. That was always his priority. Anything extra was a beachy-bonus.

He stood facing inland, surveying the terrain, soaking the light with his eyes, and planning their next move. Before them was a dewy-grassed parkland with scattered trees, and on the other side was a road. He could tell it was a road because, sprinkled down it's length, were the occasional street lamps, casting a distant light for them to aim for.

"We need to cross the park to get to the road," Boid instructed, "Follow me, and stay alert. Sometimes parks are home for stray dogs, and believe me, you can't outrun those rabid beasts. If you see one, don't try to talk to it. Keep quiet, drop to your belly, and pretend to be invisible."

Boid was speaking from experience. He was chased by a dog in a park a few years ago. He had attempted to reason with it, but some dogs are far too excitable to talk to, and have trouble controlling their instincts. At that time, the dog's instinct was to chase him. Boid's instinct was to grab a bunch of helium balloons from a nearby stall, and escape by floating away, like a mini Moonbeam Mary Poppins. But with balloons, not an umbrella.

Soon after that experience he met a Moonbeam called Shinav, who claimed he could teach the art of invisibility, and because getting eaten by a dog had never been on Boid's to-do list, he signed up for the course. He had also heard rumours that some Moonbeams had gained special abilities after so many light jumps, and was curious to see if was true.

However, when he turned up to the first invisibility lesson, Shinav wasn't there, so Boid went home and tried to forget about it. He convinced himself that he was probably just a bit of fantasist, with wild claims, and it had all been an overexcited attempt to impress him. Then, a day later he received a letter from him saying, 'See you next week for Lesson Two…Don't give up so early.' He accepted the wisdom on not giving up, but decided one lesson was enough.

Leading the way, he set off into the parkland, and the team followed tightly. The first thing to hit them was the sweet smell of the damp grass. It appeared to be regularly cut, but was still waist high to Boid. When he looked behind, he could see it was almost head high to Luna. To make her way through it, she had to use her arms to brush away the blades, as if she was swimming a breaststroke. She had steely determination in her eyes, looking focused on keeping pace.

Boid was constantly scanning the surrounding environment. He knew that being unaware of your surroundings could be calamitous for Moonbeams, and Boid wasn't a fan of calamities. He could see the street lamp ahead flicker, and then, just for a moment, he saw a tiny figure standing under it, watching them. The lamp flickered once more, and the figure was gone.

Was it a trick of the light, or had he imagined it? Were they being followed? If so, why? Who's interested in this mission, and are they friendly or hostile?

All these thoughts rushed through Boid's mind, but within a few moments they would reach the pathway, so he decided to think about it later. When they got there, Boid took a look around, saw nothing but a quiet street, then turned to face his team.

"Okay guys, good work," he said, "Now we need to get to the other side of the city," and moved to one side.

When he moved they could all see that, beyond the treetops, a sprawl of high-rise buildings scraped the sky, twinkling in the distance, like beacons. They were partially clouded in a wispy night mist, tracing across its tops, as if it was a winter breath from the city itself.

"Wow!" Luna and Fluff remarked in unison, jaws dropping in astonishment at the sight of the metropolis. Boid knew they were as impressed as he was when he first saw a human city. It was very impressive, humans were impressive. They seemed to have an ability to surpass all expectations and, each time he visited, the buildings were bigger and bolder. It really was something special.

In the distance appeared the headlights of a car, turning the corner to join the road, heading in the direction of the city. It was often remarked to him that Boid seemed always to be in the right place, at the right time. They said he was lucky, but he always said he took opportunities when they presented themselves. 'It isn't about luck, it's about a state of mind' he would respond cryptically, in the belief that the more people thought you were lucky, the more luck you would seem to have. In reality, Boid always did extensive research before each mission. He had virtually memorised the map of the city, where their destination was, and could tell if they were going in the right direction just by the position of The Moon.

"This is our ride," Boid exclaimed, "These cars have a foot cill, and we're gonna be surfing on it. When it comes by, I want you to give me your best Moonbeam leap. We only get one shot at it, so make it count. You've just had bounce practice, now it's time to make use of it!"

As the brightness of the headlights came upon them, Boid started his trot up the pathway, leaping from the curb, and onto the road.

"Come on!" he shouted.

Without hesitation, they all started to run after him, needing to gain momentum, in order to make the leap onto the car easier. Soon they were all running hard, with Boid keeping one eye on the approaching vehicle. The car was not speeding by any means but, within a few seconds, it was beside them, on the overtake. Boid saw his chance, and sprung powerfully into the air, to land gracefully onto the metal foot cill that ran along the side of the car, the long flat surface he had told them about. A skilful landing allowed him to make an instant grab for the crack of the side door, and he held on tight. As he turned his head, he saw Jipp land beside him elegantly, his big feet grabbing themselves to the metal surface, as if he had hidden suckers on them.

The cadets came leaping towards them, their expressions a mixture of determination and horror. Boid knew they were on target, so held out a hand to grab Luna, whilst Jipp made a reach for Fluff. As soon as he made contact Boid swung Luna to his side, safely onto the cill, and she dropped down to cling on as tightly as she could. He turned to see Fluff make a confident landing, mindfully eased on by Jipp's guiding hand. They were now all on, and in one piece. Boid looked at his team, saw they were safe, and allowed himself a moment to breathe out. He glanced up to check The Moon. They were headed into the city, going in the right direction, and soon to be surfing the late-night traffic.

The city hit like a thunderbolt. The smell of diesel smoke, the growl of engines, the flashing of lights, and people briskly walking from place to place. It was an assault on the senses, but also astonishing. Boid had to marvel at the ingenuity behind it all. Humans seemed to build and build, invent and improve, faster and faster, bigger and better, they just never stopped. The Man had seemed to take credit for inspiring such invention, but to lay claim to all of this? It was a bit of a stretch.

Boid looked up to see the buildings scraping the sky, with some still unfinished, cranes atop, swinging metal beams on wires. Men were sitting upon some of them, eating late-night sandwich suppers, unfazed by the precarious height. Down below, the streets were teaming with more people than Boid had ever seen. They seemed to multiply before his eyes, hustling and bustling.

If a Moonbeam was to get caught under all those feet it would not end well, Boid thought, But, we're making good progress, so just stay putt, remaining positive.

He crouched down, gripped onto the cill, and looked to his team. They took the hint and crouched down too, trying to remain as invisible as possible. Then Luna looked up at Boid.

"Commander," she said, "Are we where I think we are?"

"And where's that, cadet?" he quizzed.

"America," she immediately replied.

He smiled knowingly, held out his spare hand, like a talk show host introducing a guest,

"Welcome to the land of opportunity!" he announced.

He could see the reflection of the city lights in Luna's bedazzled eyes, as she gawped in awe. He knew all cadets had America on their wish list. It was thought of as exciting, and considered a favoured Earthonaut destination. The people here were especially receptive to the mysterious, and every Moonbeam could relate to that.

Boid looked up again, caught an assuring sight of The Moon above, faintly visible through the city smog, and was calmed by its presence. Then, out of the corner of his eye, he saw the head of a small, hooded figure peering over at them, from the roof of the car. But when he focused his gaze, the figure had gone again.

Wait. Who was that? Was that another Moonbeam? Someone is following us. What do they want?

Before he could give it any more thought, the car screeched to a sudden halt, forcing him to concentrate on holding on. There was the sound of running footsteps, a car door being opened, a bounce of the car's suspension, a door slam, then a human scream,

"Go, go, go!"

The car squealed off, accelerating fast, and Boid had to hold so tightly it instantly felt as if his knuckles were on fire. Within moments the burning sensation was accompanied by the sound of distant sirens.

He looked back and yelled to his team, "Hold on, this could get a little choppy!"

"Get a move on, it's the cops," the passenger raved.

It wasn't quite light speed, but it was much more perilous. They were hitching a ride on a getaway car and, as the sirens got louder, the car continued to accelerate. The team plugged as tightly as they could to the rough steel foot plate, its rusty ridges helping their grip. Boid looked up quickly, gauged The Moon's position, and noticed that they were still heading in the direction of their target.

He glanced back to see a flash of siren lights behind them as the cop car started to gain on them and, seeing a break in the oncoming traffic, had started to pull alongside them. Suddenly, the car to veered to the left, cutting in front of the chasing police. The cop car pulled back to avoid collision, and held position behind them once more. His team were doing as he asked so no one lost hold by the swerve, but when he looked ahead Boid could see they were approaching an oncoming cross-road.

"Run the road!" bellowed a voice from inside the car.

As they screamed across the junction a car whizzed across them from the left, scraping past the rear of the car, and missing them by the thickness of its chrome paint bumper. Looking behind them, Boid could see that the cop car behind wasn't as fortunate. With a deafening crunch, it knifed into the rear end of another passing car from the right, spinning them both around in circles, eventually coming to a stop, in a cloud of black tyre smoke. Boid could to see the drivers of both cars get out, seemingly unharmed, bunching fists in dismay.

"Ha, ha, ha," came a laugh from inside the car, "That's ma boy!"

Then Boid saw another cop car appear from a side street, turn on its light siren, and pick up the chase once again. The car started to speed up, and began swerving through the traffic once more. Boid felt the swing violently, and his body rocked sideways, stinging his clenched hand on the door gap. The car swerved back, slamming him into side of the car, but he soaked it up, and checked to see if they had lost anyone. They had all remained flat to the metal surface, and were all still aboard, looking at him wide-eyed. He liked to make missions quick, but perhaps not this quick. Although it was fortunate the current escape route was taking them the right way, he would've preferred a less stressful ride. Glancing skyward he saw the comforting Moon and realised;

We're almost at our mission destination already.

"Everyone okay?" he said, looking back.

They all nodded unconvincingly.

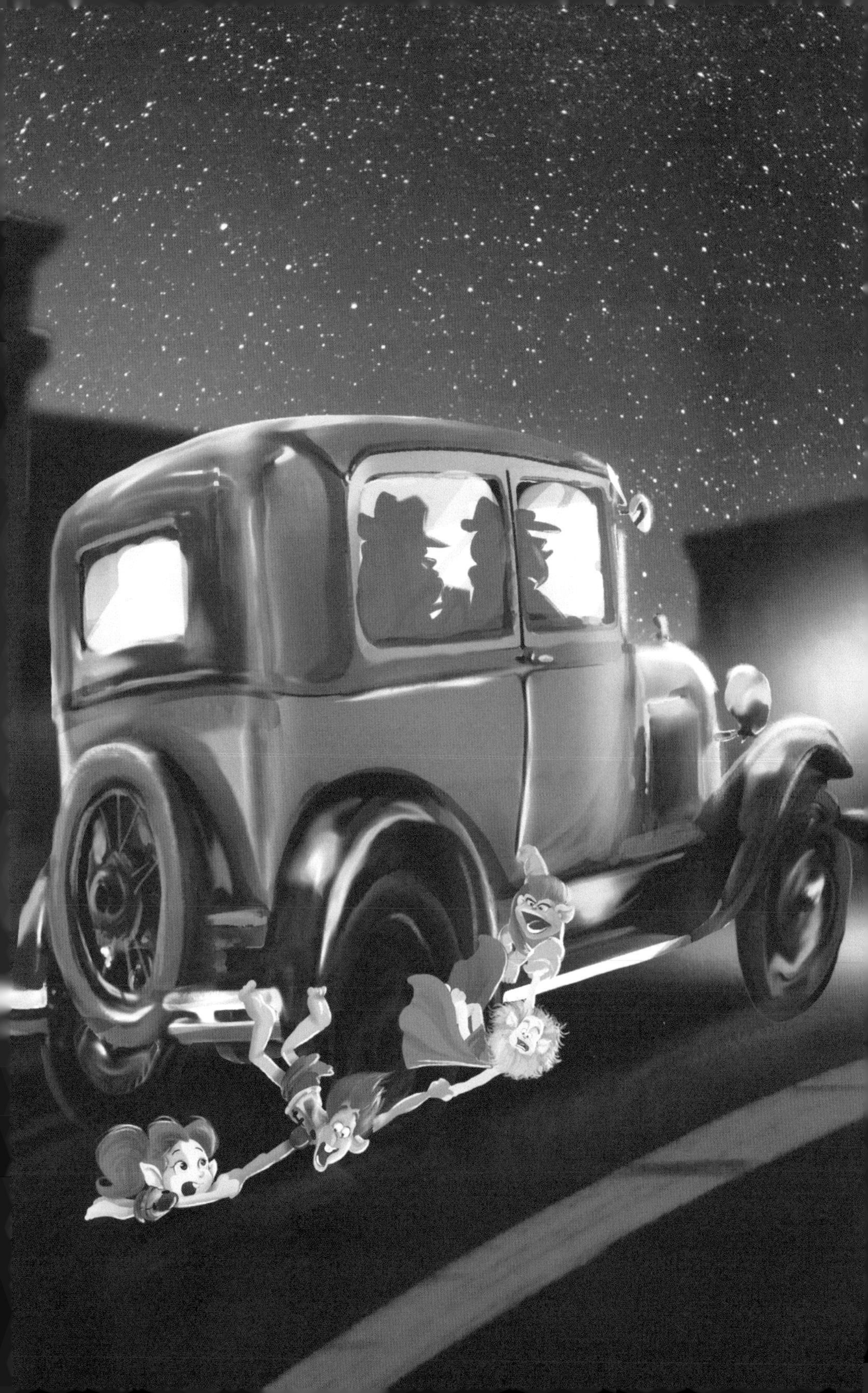

"Just a little while longer," he attempted to reassure them.

Then the human voice cried, "Make a turn! Turn here, and we'll lose 'em."

The tyres squealed, and the car made a rapid turn left. The left wheels lifted from the road, tilting the car. Luna lost her grip on the cill, and flew backwards, knocking Fluff off his feet. As Luna tumbled past Fluff she made a desperate grasp for something to wrap her arms around, and found Fluff's trailing right leg. With the reactions of a fly, Jipp shot out his hand to grab Fluff's wrist, and held on so tight it was as if he was trying to melt their arms together. Boid immediately took his free arm and wrapped it with Jipp's, to help take the strain of the line. They were linked together, pulled horizontally outwards, like a Moonbeam daisy chain, flapping helplessly in the wind.

"Hold on tight!" cried Boid.

As the car straightened up, they were swung back towards the side of the car. Luna whipped in with the most force and hit the metal hard. The impact on her arms knocked them free from her grip on Fluff's leg, and she was tossed helplessly into the air. Boid could only watch, as he witnessed his worst nightmare.

With abject terror in her eyes, she screamed, 'Aaaaaaarrrrgh!'

In the opposite direction, on the other side of the road, came the startling headlights of a large oil truck heading straight for her powerless, spinning body.

"LUNA!" cried Fluff.

In just a moment it was over, the truck sped away into the distance, but Luna was nowhere to be seen. Boid looked back, eyes glazed, hoping that, somehow, it hadn't happened.

Was there any way of surviving that sort of impact?

The sirens sounds had started to quieten, and the car pulled into a side street. It came to a stop, and the driver turned off the engine and lights. After a few seconds the noise of sirens seemed to pass them by. Then there was silence. A deafening, crushing, nauseating silence. They all had just witnessed the death of a team member, and everything was lost.

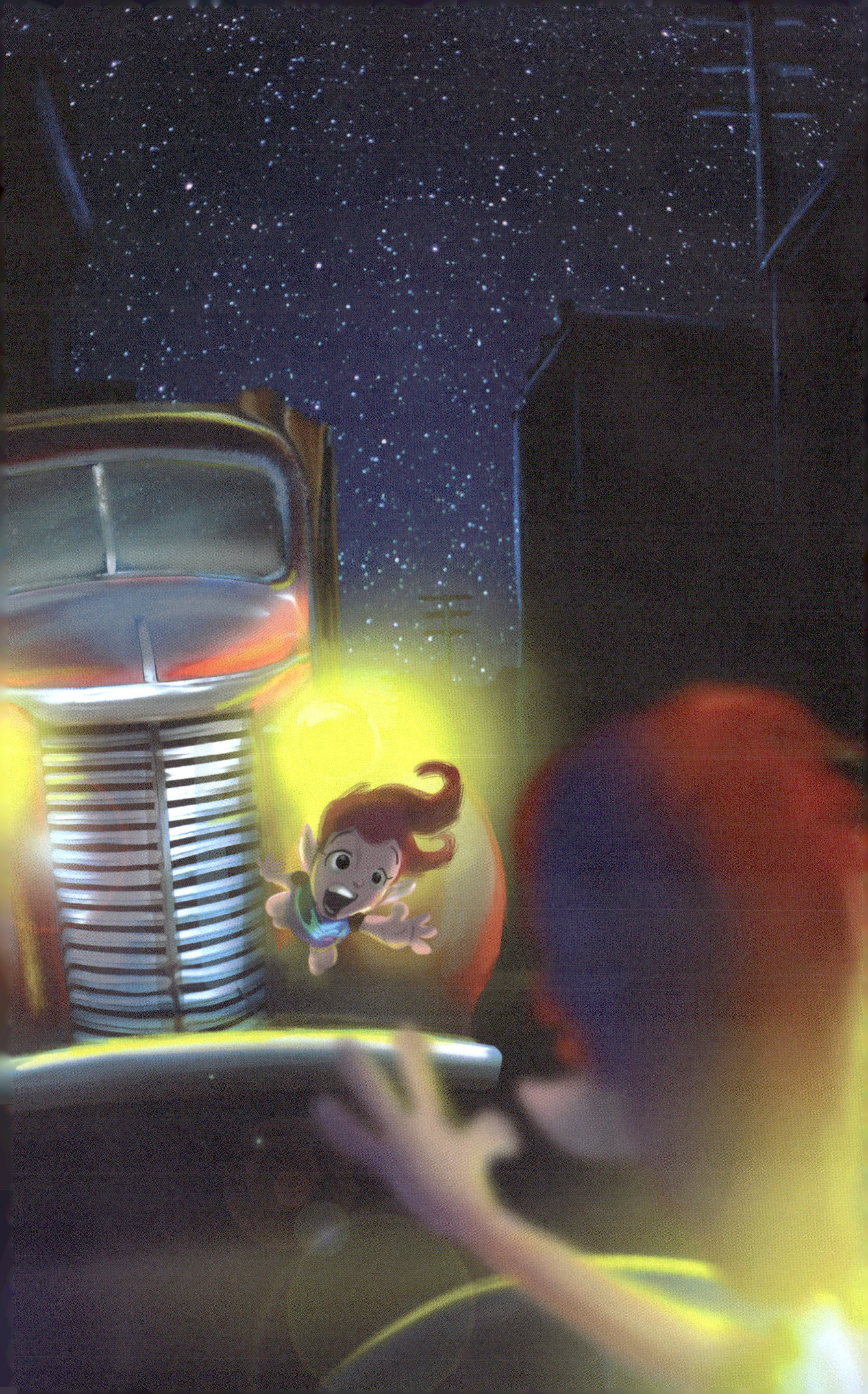

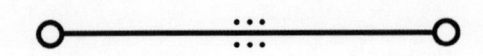

CHAPTER FOUR:
FALLEN HEROES

"Noooooooo!" sobbed Fluff, dropping to his knees.

Boid could only assume that the impact of the truck would have been fatal, and the thought of it made his stomach churn. Losing an Earthonaut was a Commander's worst nightmare, and losing this promising Earthonaut was especially hard to take. She was spirited, and he had taken an instant liking to her. He could sense her promise, and the loss of such promise caused a sickening shudder to echo through his bones. However, their position was compromised, and he needed to focus on the safety of the rest of his team. Fluff's cries could be overheard, and that could put them in danger once again. He motioned to Jipp, and they both moved to his side. They took an arm each, and lifted him up. Boid leaned towards Fluff's ear and said,

"We've got to go, cadet. It's not safe,"

Taking charge of him, Boid and Jipp made a timed leap from the cill, and all three landed on the pavement.

"Take cover in those bushes, over there," Boid instructed, pointing to a nearby scrub bed on the other side of the path. Fluff was still quietly weeping, as they both dragged him to the undergrowth. When they were hidden, they let go of his arms. Fluff fell to his knees, put his head in his hands, and started to blubber uncontrollably.

"Why?" Fluff cried, "She was so young!"

Boid looked at Jipp, and he looked back. His stunned face offered no words, and they turned to stand silently, staring at the car in disbelief.

"Did you hear something?" said the human passenger to the driver.

"Huh?" he replied.

"Over there," he said, pointing out of the driver window, "I thought I heard something."

The driver slowly lifted up, peered out of the window, and flicked his eyes around. His gaze found their direction for a moment, so Boid dropped to the ground. Jipp immediately did the same.

"Shhh!" Boid whispered to Fluff.

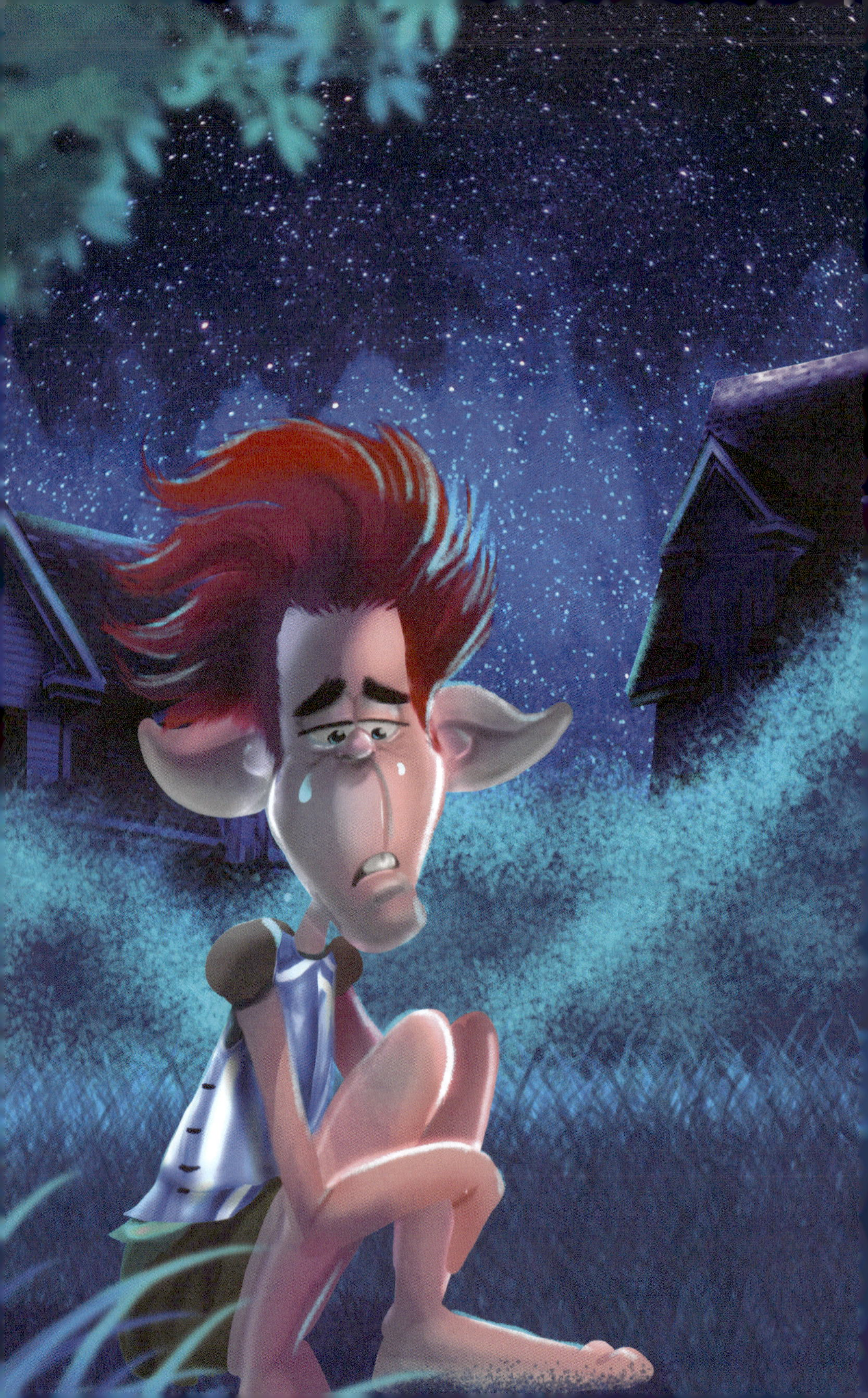

Fluff held his breath the best he could, and they froze solid, hoping the darkness of the shrubbery was enough.

"There ain't nothin' there," the driver said.

"Must've been a cat or something," concluded the passenger, "Let's get outta here."

The driver lifted up in his seat, turned the ignition, and revved the engine. Boid watched the car forlornly, as it accelerated away, leaving behind a black cloud of exhaust fumes spinning in the night breeze. The sound of the city seemed to fade to nothing, as if it itself was offering a minute's silence, in shared sorrow.

Boid wasn't sure what to do next. Protocol meant that the mission came first, but he didn't feel he had the heart to continue. Fluff was sat with his head still in his hands, quietly blubbing, when Jipp looked to Boid.

"Time to go home, buddy," Jipp said.

Boid took a gulp, and answered,

"But, what about the mission?"

"Forget the mission, let's go home. We can't go on in these circumstances," Jipp reasoned.

Boid just stared back, blankly.

He was right. How could they complete the mission after such a dreadful loss?

His mind raced to the moment he was going to have to tell her family, and his stomach-churn went up a notch.

What would he tell them? How could he say the words?

Luna is dead; A promising Earthonaut tragically killed in action, on her first ever mission. A mission she had waited her entire life to go on. A mission he was responsible for. He was the one pushing them. They could have got there safer, but he chose the daring option, the fast option. He couldn't stop thinking,

Was it my ambition that was responsible? Had I pushed them too far, in an effort to show off? Had I gotten too reckless? How would The Man react? What would my parents think of me? He wouldn't be able to take mother to Fiji now.

All these thoughts crowded his mind, some of them he was guilty of thinking, and the belly-churning hit spin-cycle nine. He was just about to lose his lunch, when Jipp's voice called him back,

"Boid?" he said, "Earthonaut to Boid? Come in, Commander."

Boid gazed back at him with no words.

"Are we going home, or what?" Jipp quizzed.

"No, we are not," Fluff stated firmly. He had stopped crying, wiped his eyes, and had stood up.

"If we go home now, Luna will have died for nothing," Fluff continued, "We do it for her. We complete the mission for her."

Boid looked him in those pained, puffy eyes, and he could that tell he meant every word. Jipp raised that eyebrow again, but this time it meant, you can't really argue with that. Boid knew their destination was only down the street, and they could still do the mission with three, but he wasn't sure he or his team would be in the right mind to do it.

Then Fluff stepped forwards pleadingly,

"Please Commander. She was my friend," he said, wearing the expression that no one says no to.

"Okay. We do it to honour her," Boid replied, "Follow me. Our destination is only down the road."

He stepped forwards, heading out from the scrub bed, and began striding purposefully down the street. Jipp and Fluff looked to each other, gathered themselves, and sombrely followed after him. Boid knew that it would soon be time to reveal what the mission actually was.

CHAPTER FIVE:
THE SOCK OF GREAT IMPORTANCE

The sound of the city seemed far away, as they had turned down a quiet, suburban street, comfortably lit by The Moon and just a few street lamps. They had reached their target objective, and Boid knew it was time to brief the team. He led them to a mailbox, standing discreetly behind some shrubs, on a nearby front lawn, and gathered them together. They both looked at him, waiting for the big reveal.

"Now, I'm sure you're both wondering what our mission actually is," he said.

Fluff silently nodded, but Jipp's face looked as if he had already guessed.

"Our mission is that house across the street," Boid said, pointing to a property over the road.

They turned their heads to look.

The house was lit by a lone street lamp, which made the house stand out at night, and was clad in horizontal green timber boarding. On its front elevation were two lit windows on the ground floor, three windows on the first floor, and two dormer windows in the sloping, grey tiled roof. The garden path led up to the front door in the middle, served by a grand stepped porch, timber posts either side holding up the front balcony above. Partially obscuring its frontage was a large crooked tree, with its trunk split in the middle, like a two-pronged, knobbly wooden fork with leaves.

"In that house lives a very special young boy," he said, "And we need to retrieve one of his socks,"

Fluff stared blankly at him, and Jipp let out a little sigh.

"I don't understand," said Fluff, "We're here to get a sock?"

"Yes. A sock," replied Boid, "A sock of great importance."

"I knew it," tutted Jipp.

"A sock?" asked Fluff, scornfully, "All this for a sock?"

Boid knew The Man had a thing for stealing children's socks, and knew a lot of Moonbeams thought it was a waste of time. He also knew that Jipp thought the mystery of a missing sock was dull and pointless. Who cared where missing socks had got to? It was so much more fun to pretend to be a poltergeist, or something.

No great story had ever come from a sock mission. It just wasn't considered a glamorous gig. He knew that perhaps they might have been expecting the mission to be a little bit more spectacular, and felt the need to address their probable disappointment. If truth be told, Boid himself was hoping for a more thrilling mission. Stealing socks was entry-level stuff.

Don't tell them that though. Dress it up a bit, he thought.

"What is the greatest human mystery ever?" Boid asked him.

Fluff paused for thought and replied, "Life, the universe, and everything?"

"I'll tell you," Boid explained, ignoring him, "It's the loss of one of your socks."

This is where you earn your stripes, Boid thought.

"Forget playing poltergeist, socks are where it's at. Throughout history it has been a mystery for both young, and old. They all say 'Where's my sock gone? Where do they get to?' It's baffled them for centuries. It creates a starting point for a child to have an open mind, and helps distract from life's worries. Try not to forget that this is the start of everything for this boy, it's the beginning of his life of wonder, and we're all going to be part of that."

Boid tried to remember some of what The Man had said,

"What we do, no matter how small, can cause ripples. Ripples in pond. A time pond."

Or something like that, he thought.

"So, we're gonna get that sock, we're gonna do it for Luna, and it's gonna be the best darn sock theft in the history of Moonkind. Are you with me?"

"Yes sir!" Fluff cried enthusiastically.

"Excellent," said Boid, making a relieved move to cross the road, "Let's go. It's sock time."

As they made their way up to the front garden path, he scoped the house for a point of entry. He first looked to see if the front door had a cat flap, but it didn't. Looking up, he saw the right ground-floor sash window was slightly open, the lights were on, and there was a faint sound of music coming from inside. When

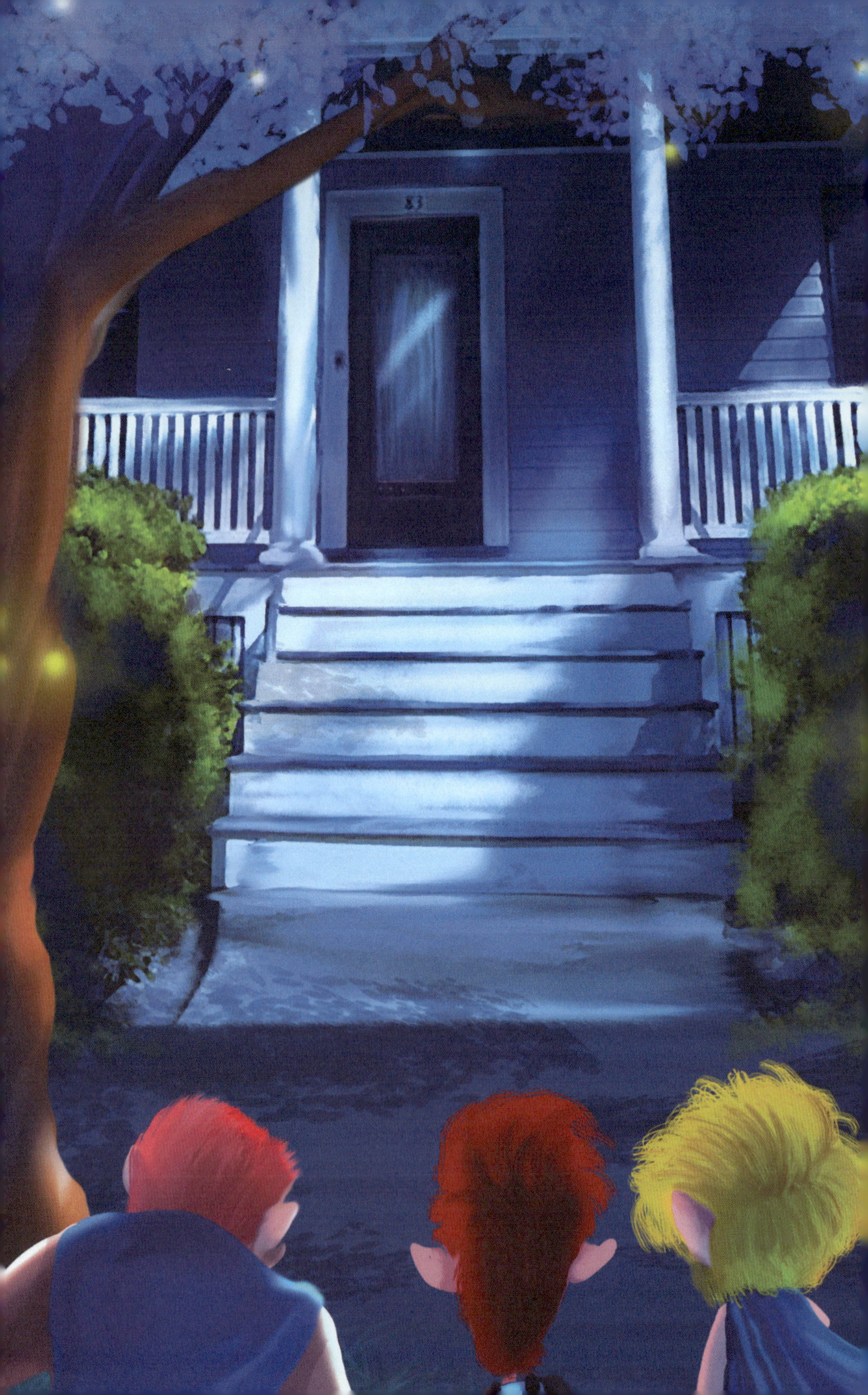

they reached the steps to the front door, he stopped, and turned to face the team.

"Okay. Now, the plan is this; We go up the steps, onto the porch, climb up the porch balustrade, and onto the rail," he said, pointing upwards, "Then jump to the cill and through the open ground floor window,"

Then, from somewhere above them, came an unfamiliar voice,

"I wouldn't do that if I were you…"

CHAPTER SIX:
THE EARTHTIMER

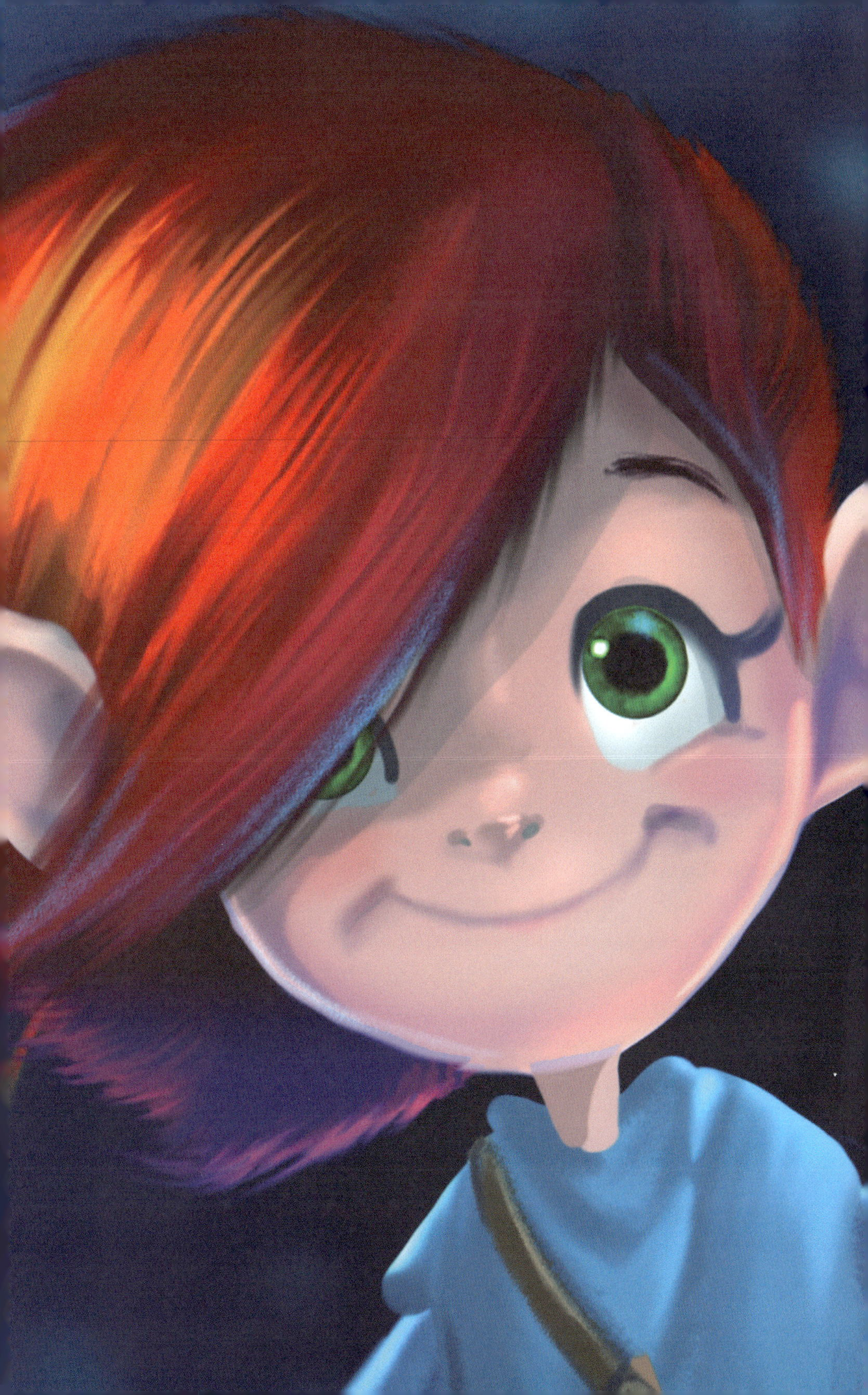

"...Not unless you wanna get eaten by rabid dogs," The team all looked up, in the direction of the voice, to see a small figure in a hooded cape, sat nonchalantly, on the porch handrail. It was as if she had appeared from nowhere. Boid couldn't quite see the face, because of the hood, but he could immediately tell it was the mysterious Moonbeam he had seen earlier. What he also couldn't fail to notice, was the word dogs.

Dogs. Oh please, not dogs.

"They have more than one, you know. They're everywhere. Good luck making your way through that lot," the hooded Moonbeam added.

Boid was intrigued by the information, but unexpectedly annoyed by the interference. It was his mission, his command, and it was a strange mixed feeling. Then she lifted her head and he noticed her piercing emerald eyes, so bright it was as if they shone. Immediately he realised she was a Moonbeam that lived on Earth for good, and one of only a handful across the globe. Her eyes had turned that colour due to sun exposure, and she was one of them. An Earthtimer.

"Have you been following us?" Boid asked.

The Earthtimer leapt to her feet, sprung backwards from the rail, acrobatically somersaulting down to the porch deck, and landed with an impressive ninja role, at the top of the porch steps. Then she stood tall, flipped back her hood, and confidently faced them. Boid could see she had skills, was impressed, and could instantly sense the team were impressed too.

"Of course," she replied, "And it's a good job. You wouldn't have got here without me. So far, you've cost me a crate of molluscs," she revealed, "So believe me when I say; Go that way, and you'll never even make it to The Boy's sock drawer," she said.

Boid had no idea what she meant by the molluscs, but then did a double-take,

"Wait a minute! What do you know about The Boy?" he asked, "What do you know about our mission?"

"I know about lots of things," she answered knowingly.

As she talked she began to creep slinkily down the steps

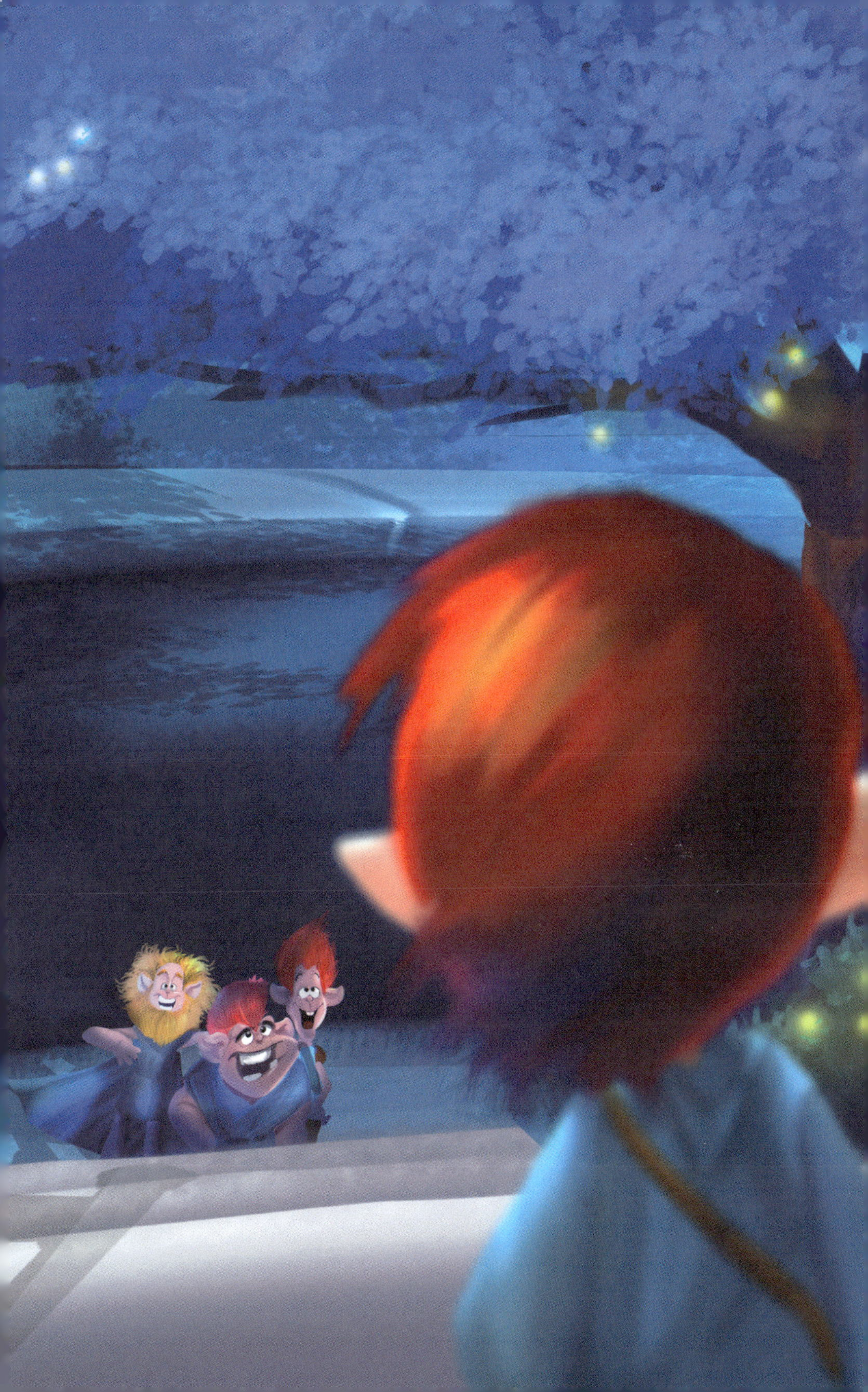

towards them. When the lamplight caught her figure, he could see the cape swish aside, to reveal a hidden satchel strapped over her shoulder. He could only guess what she had in there. Her face oozed pure confidence, as she looked them all up and down, with darting eyes so bright they were hard to look at. She clearly had local knowledge, and obvious talent, so Boid knew he should hear her out.

"One other thing I know, is that his bedroom is on the top floor, which is why you need a better plan. A Plan B, if you will."

"And you have such a plan?" Boid prompted.

Without words, the Earthtimer started to walk down the path towards the crooked tree. When she reached it, she turned and looked upwards.

"There," she said, "Up there,"

"Where?"

"The tree," she replied, "You climb this tree,"

"But the tree is over there, and the house is over here. Wrong direction," gasped Boid.

"Yes, but this gnarly old tree happens to go in a few different directions," she added, "And one of its forks runs under your boy's bedroom window. A window that just so happens to be a few inches open."

Boid immediately stepped away from the house, turned, and craned his neck to glare upwards. The left branch did indeed shoot off toward the house, and its thinnest branches skirted a tantalising distance from the top dormer window, left ever so slightly open. The branches, however, were a little on the thin side, and it seemed a risky leap. He thought it could possibly be do-able; if they were bats, or squirrels, or bat-squirrels. He couldn't help feel a tad disappointed, somehow he expected a more rounded plan.

"Look. I appreciate the information, I really do, but it's too far," Boid said, "We won't make it."

"You will if you use this," she replied, reaching inside her cloak.

She pulled out a loop of strange looking wire from her satchel, "This was made especially. It's my last one, but I'll let you use it. It can easily take the weight of a Moonbeam," she smiled as she spoke.

"What's it made from?" Fluff couldn't help but ask.

"It's woven from thousands of high tensile spider webs. It was a gift," she replied.

"From spiders?" Fluff quizzed.

"Yes."

"You have spider friends?"

"Sure, I do."

"But, aren't they a bit....y'know?"

"Hard to talk to?" The Earthtimer replied.

"I heard that their language sounds like sarcastic laughter."

"Yeah, it does at first, but after a while you start to hear actual words."

Boid could remember hearing about the famous diplomatic mission to foster relations with the spiders. It was known as Arachnid Friday, and it didn't quite go to plan. The Moonbeam envoy tried to compliment the spiders on how useful it must be to have all of those legs, but it came out sounding sarcastic. The spiders sounded just as sarcastic in response, and talks went downhill from there. It was the reason Fluff appeared so surprised to hear of a Moonbeam-spider alliance. It was also the reason why most spiders mainly just teased moonbeams for only having two legs, like it was running joke they all sarcastically shared.

"Okay," Boid declared, "It's as good a plan as any. It's a plan that avoids dogs, and that's good enough for me."

The Earthtimer smiled once more.

"Just one more thing…" she said, "A little while earlier I think I found something of yours," and jumped back up the steps she had walked down, just moments earlier.

Boid turned around to look, and could not believe his eyes.
WHAT?

"Hey guys," Luna said, standing there boldly, "Did you miss me?" and she flashed her beaming smile.

When Fluff saw her he screamed, "LUNA!" and he charged up the steps towards her. He wrapped his arms around

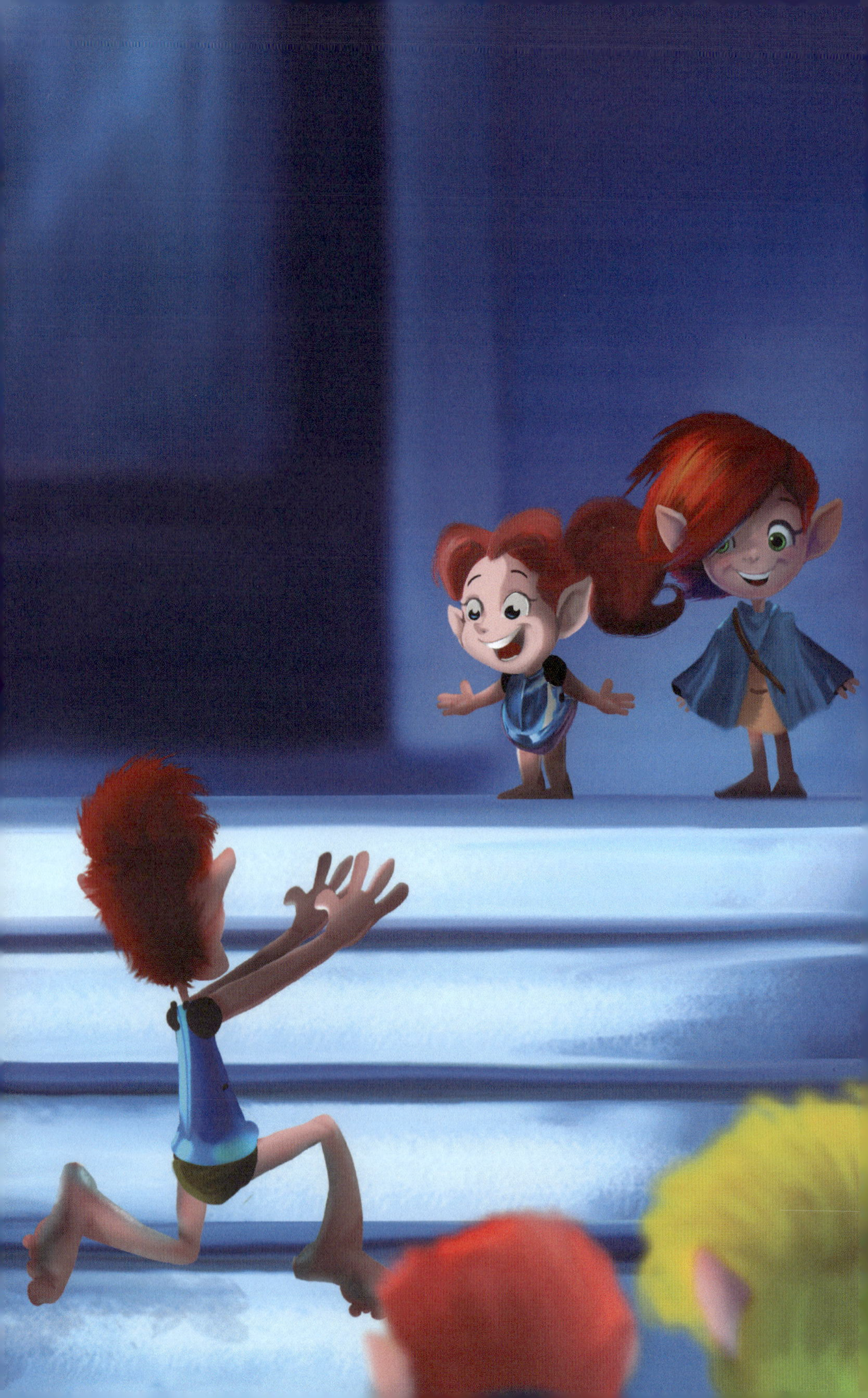

her and squeezed her so tight he lifted her off the floor. He spun her around, and let go. Holding his hand on her shoulders, his expression turned from relief to confusion.

"But how?" he questioned, "We thought…"

"I'd been squished?" she interrupted.

"Well, yes. What happened?" Fluff asked.

"I was millimetres away from it," Luna said, "But a split second before the truck hit me I felt the spider-wire loop around my leg, and was swung away. I landed on the back bumper of the car, and hit it so hard I blacked out. The next thing I knew I woke up at the side of the road, with a pair of bright green eyes looking down at me."

Boid had never felt so relieved. With his shoulders instantly feeling lighter, he turned to The Earthtimer to thank her. But she wasn't waiting around for gratitude, she had already jumped up onto the tree trunk. Then, as if she was descended from spiders herself, she grabbed onto the knobbly bark, and scuttled expertly up it. Boid looked at Luna, and smiled.

"Nice illusion cadet," he said, "I appreciate the theatre. Bit dark for my tastes, but I'm glad you're still with us," he attempted to make light of it, even though inside he was absolutely elated.

"Well, you heard the lady," he said to the team, "Go climb that tree."

An inspired Jipp was first to take an athletic jump. The moment he hit the trunk it seemed like his long toes had wrapped themselves around it, and he scrambled upwards, like a hungry gecko after a fly on the ceiling. Then, the cadets followed his lead, and started making their way, enthusiastically upwards. Boid took a look up, saw the team reach the fork in the tree, and started the climb himself.

As he was making his way up the forked branch, he could see the Earthtimer was already balanced expertly on the end of it. She reached for the wire and began whirling the loop around her head, like a five-inch-tall cowboy. Her eyes were focused on the pointed roof of their target dormer window, The Boy's window. As the lasso reached an impressive width, she flicked her wrists, and

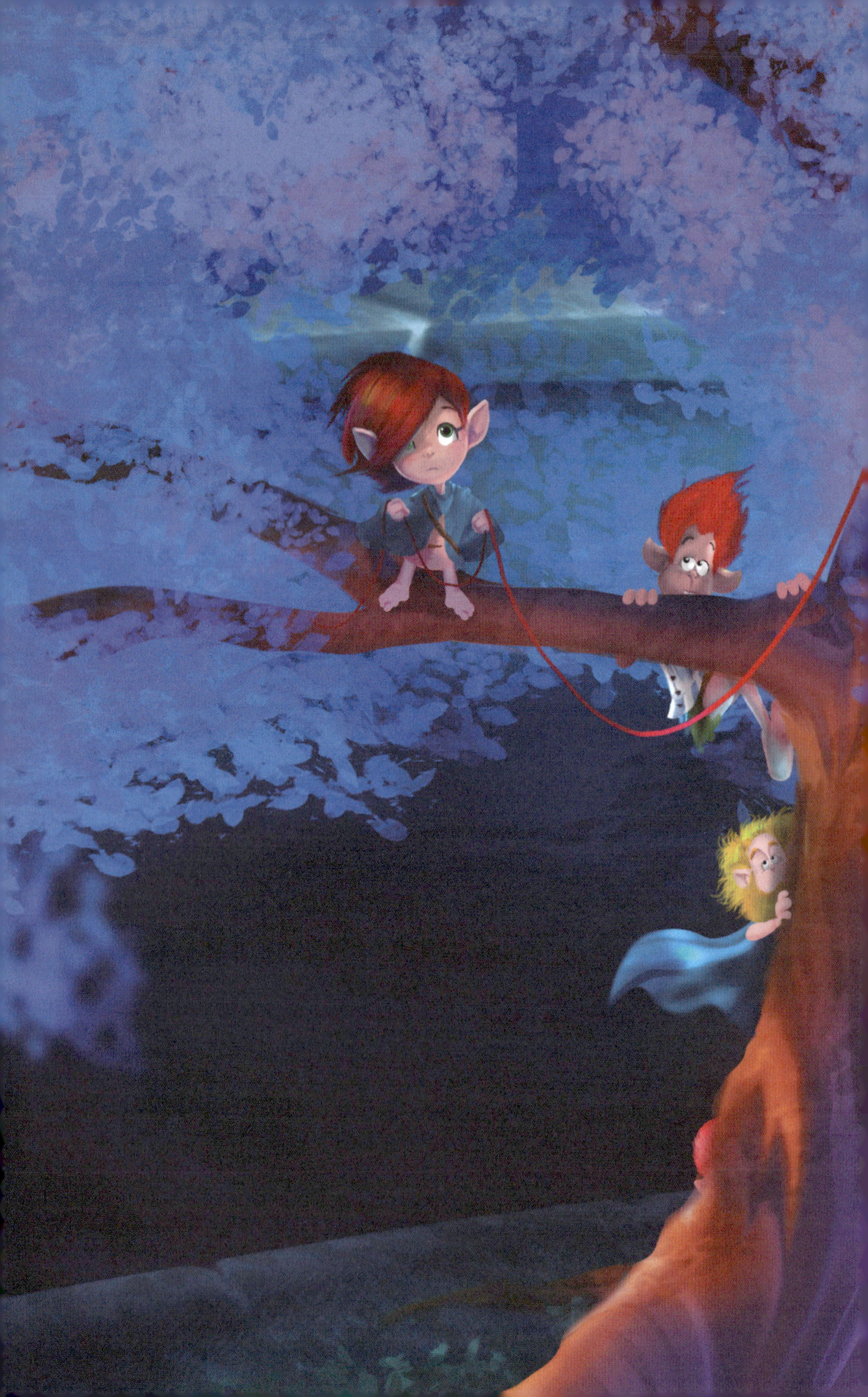

whipped it upwards with just as impressive a speed. It hooked over first time and, in one movement, she tugged it tight. Then she took the end, and wrapped it around the branch she stood upon. There was a momentary bounce, a rustle of leaves, and the Earthtimer turned to face them all.

With a smile, she said, "Now it's sock time."

The team had all reached the join of the branch, and were looking at her with awe.

She is quite something, Boid thought, and by the look on Luna's face, she thought so too. The Earthtimer casually sauntered back across the branch and squeezed herself, cat-like, past the team, to take position behind them. She sat down, pulled her hood forward, and offered no further comment.

"Okay, we go one at a time," said Boid.

"I'll do it first," an inspired-looking Luna immediately declared, starting to make her way up the branch, without waiting for a response.

CHAPTER SEVEN:
SKIN OF THE HOUND'S TEETH

Standing with toes gripped tight against the bark, Luna stared intensely up the line of wire. She took a breath and then grabbed it. With one confident leap, she wrapped her legs around it, and spun to a hanging position. The wire tightened under her weight, and she started pulling herself up with one hand, and then the other, over and over, until she started to reach a solid rhythm.

With pride, Boid was silently cheering her on. He was watching someone who took life by the scruff of the neck, and he liked that. He saw an inspired, capable Earthonaut, with a great attitude, and he liked that too. If truth be told, he'd taken a bit of a shine to her indomitable spirit.

Strangely, he felt the need to glance back at the Earthtimer to share the victory, but when he did, he saw that she had mysteriously vanished. Typical, true to form, and the type of sign-off he sort of expected.

When Boid looked back, Luna had almost made the halfway mark. The wire started to dip in the middle, dangling her above the first-floor balcony, but she was doing well, and keeping a machine-like pace. When he took a look down from his position on the branch, he could see that the window he thought he saw from the street, was in-fact a glass door that led out onto the balcony. What was worse was the fact that it was slightly open, and there was a whisper of light coming from inside. Boid immediately felt his heart drop.

What if there's a dog lurking in there? At best a barking dog could ruin everything, at worst Luna could be in danger once again. He had already lost her once, he didn't want lose her again.

No. Trust The Earthtimer's knowledge, he thought.

He took an anxious look at Luna, and was pleased to see she was still doing a pretty good spider impression. Then, there was the sound of a snort from the open crack in the door, and Boid's worst fears were realised.

Paws grabbed at the door….

She said we would avoid the dogs?

The door sprung wide open, and out bounded a hound, all slaver mouthed, with the hunt in his eyes. He didn't look like he was in the mood for a chat, and was heading right for Luna. Boid's stomach turned in on itself with a cold dread. He wanted to call, but Fluff beat him to it.

"Luna!" he yelled, "Watch out!"

The Hound took a few steps across the deck and hurled himself into the air, snapping his jaws at Luna, with just inches to spare. With its growling breath below, it startled her into lifting up her body. Her legs quivered, and unravelled from around the wire, swinging her body down, and she hung by her hands with throttled grip as the wire swung sideways. The Hound hit the deck in heap, and let out a pained squeal.

Dogs always did that; leap first, then think later, thought Boid.

It was why he wasn't a fan of them. It's not easy to think later when you're inside the belly of a dog.

The Hound arose, snarled and, from a standing start, began to leap again, all gruntingly sharp-toothed and snorting.

"Luna!" Cried Fluff, "Pull up! Pull up!"

Boid needed to do something.

Should I cut the line? It would swing her toward the wall of the house, and away from The Hound, if I timed it just right, he thought.

But before he could do anything he saw a ball bouncing down the sloped roof of the house. It flew over the gutter and hit the balcony deck. On landing, it let out a squeak, and bounced some more. It immediately grabbed The Hound's attention. A squeaky bouncing ball, what dog could resist? He stopped jumping, turned, and charged straight for it. He pounced, snapped his jaws around it, pinned it down, and started to gnaw on it with gleeful ferocity, rejoicing in the irritating sound of the squeak.

Boid looked over at Luna to see her swing her legs up, and wrap them warmly around the wire. She took a huge breath, then started to pull again, hand over hand, up the line, like a true professional.

Boid wondered where the ball had come from, and when he looked up, he spied a familiar hooded figure stood on the ridge of the roof. With the The Moon filling the sky behind her, The Earthtimer was silhouetted like a hooded angel, her cape gently flapping in the evening breeze. She had been watching, knew they needed help, and had thrown the ball. Plan C.

Very smart, he thought.

Then, in the blink of an eye, she was gone, all mysterious-like. As always, Boid appreciated the theatre.

When he looked back, Luna had progressed quickly and was now hanging over the roof guttering. Seeing the opportunity to drop, she let her legs go, and swung down feet first, then let her hands go, to land safely in the cup of the gutter. For a few moments there was nothing but the sound of the squeaky ball and a satisfied growl. Then Luna shot up to wave her arms in a silent victory dance.

Great going, Firecracker.

Boid turned to Fluff and said, "You have to go now, while The Hound is occupied."

Fluff nodded compliantly, but Boid could sense his nerves.

"It's okay, we can make it," he reassured, "But we gotta get a wriggle on."

Fluff stood up, took a gulp, and crept silently up the branch. When he got to the wire he gripped it firmly, and took the plunge. As he jumped he wrapped his ankles around the line and hung. His arms and legs were longer, and he was bigger, so the line hung lower than it did for Luna. To Boid it seemed to have stretched a little, and that put Fluff in an even more vulnerable position. He glanced over to see The Hound still chomping and squeaking, otherwise distracted. His gaze turned to watch Fluff's progress, and inside his head he started screaming,

GO! GO! GO!

Fluff's climbing technique was solid under the circumstances, and he was keeping his cool. He was exhibiting a similar focus, even more impressive considering what they had just seen. Boid looked again at The Hound. He was still happily chewing on the ball.

Then the ball stopped squeaking.

The Hound took a few more test bites to make sure, and then lost interest. He looked up, and saw Fluff dangling temptingly low enough to grab. He grunted, reared up, dropped the ball, and headed for Fluff. Boid knew this time he was the one who had to act. The Hound could jump higher at a run, meaning Fluff was in

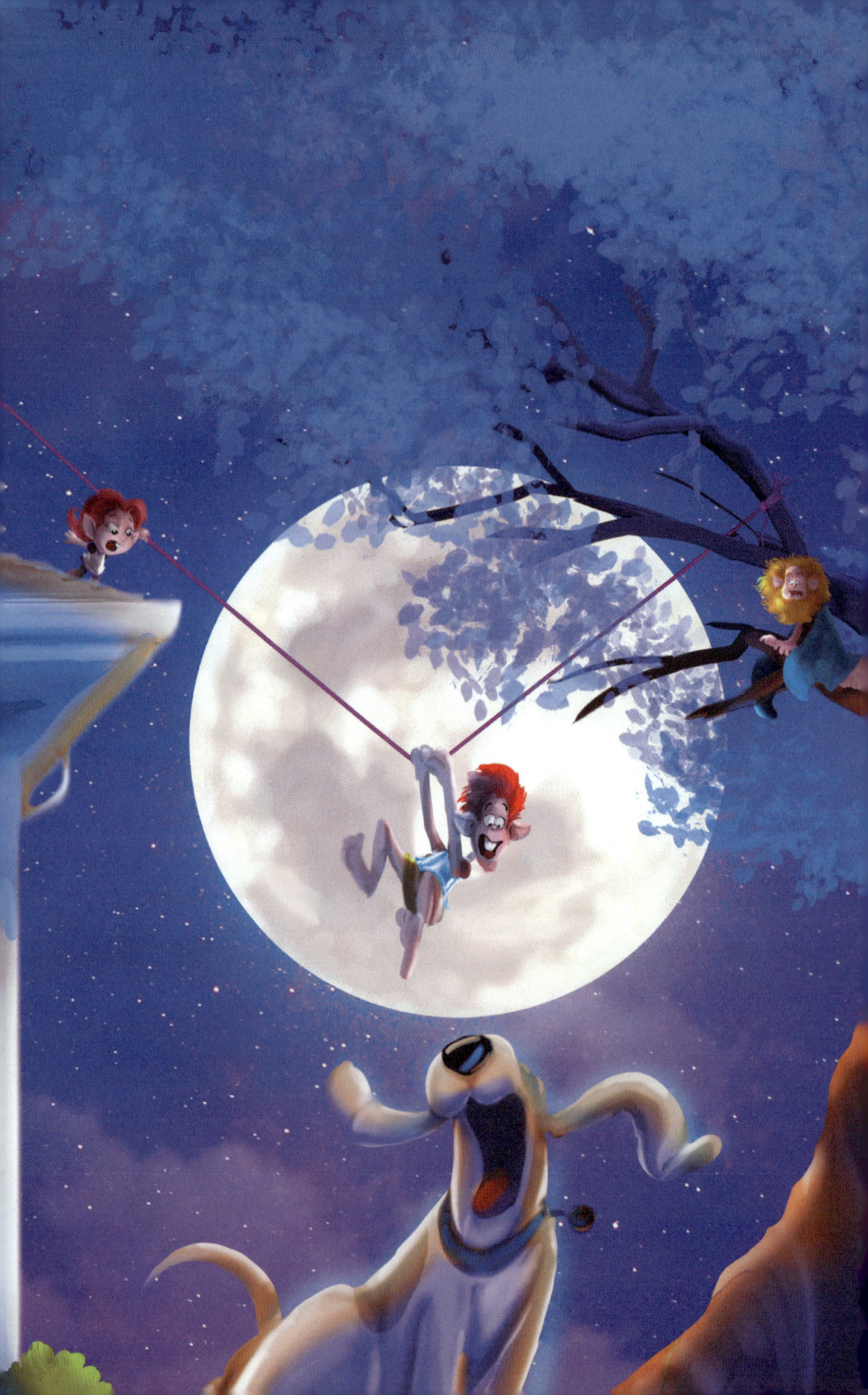

big danger.

"Cut the line! Unwrap it! Quickly," cried Jipp.

Making a leap onto the branch, Boid spread his toes, and scrambled up toward the tied wire. He dove forwards, grabbed the end of the wire, and unwrapped it speedily from the branch. Then, as The Hound leapt up ferociously, he whipped the end of the wire towards the ground.

"HOLD ON!" he yelled.

The wire immediately slackened, and Fluff clung tightly. He dropped in the air as The Hound's slavering, fang-toothed mouth passed him by. The Hound snapped his jaws shut, missing his dangling leg by a whisker, and blasting out foul dog-breath. He swung out of the way, and towards the outside wall of the house. Boid lay clinging to the branch, gawping helplessly, as Fluff hit the house wall with a dull thud. He bounced back off the wall, and when he swung back a second time he recovered, landing feet first. He was wearing his armour, and it had helped absorb the shock. Then Fluff immediately pulled hard on the wire, hand over hand, scuttling up the face, all wide-toed and urgent.

When The Hound missed his mark, he flew across the deck, and came crashing down on the balcony handrail. There a was crunch and a deafening yelp, as he bounced off the rail, and landed on his back. He gave out a second, more sheepish squeal in pain, as he lay spread eagled, humbled on the deck. As Fluff got to a safe height, he looked down to see The Hound was floored, and puffed out his cheeks to signal his relief.

Luna had taken the wire in her hands, and started to tug with all her might. She pulled and pulled, bit by bit, and wrenched her friend upwards. Fluff swung out, dangled from the under the gutter, and the last few feet were a painstaking heave to the top.

"Hey boy, what's going on out there?" came a human voice from inside.

Boid hung low, and signalled to Jipp to get down. He fell to the branch, causing it to wobble, and rustle the leaves. Then, a smartly dressed human man appeared from inside the door, stepped out onto the deck, and headed for The Hound.

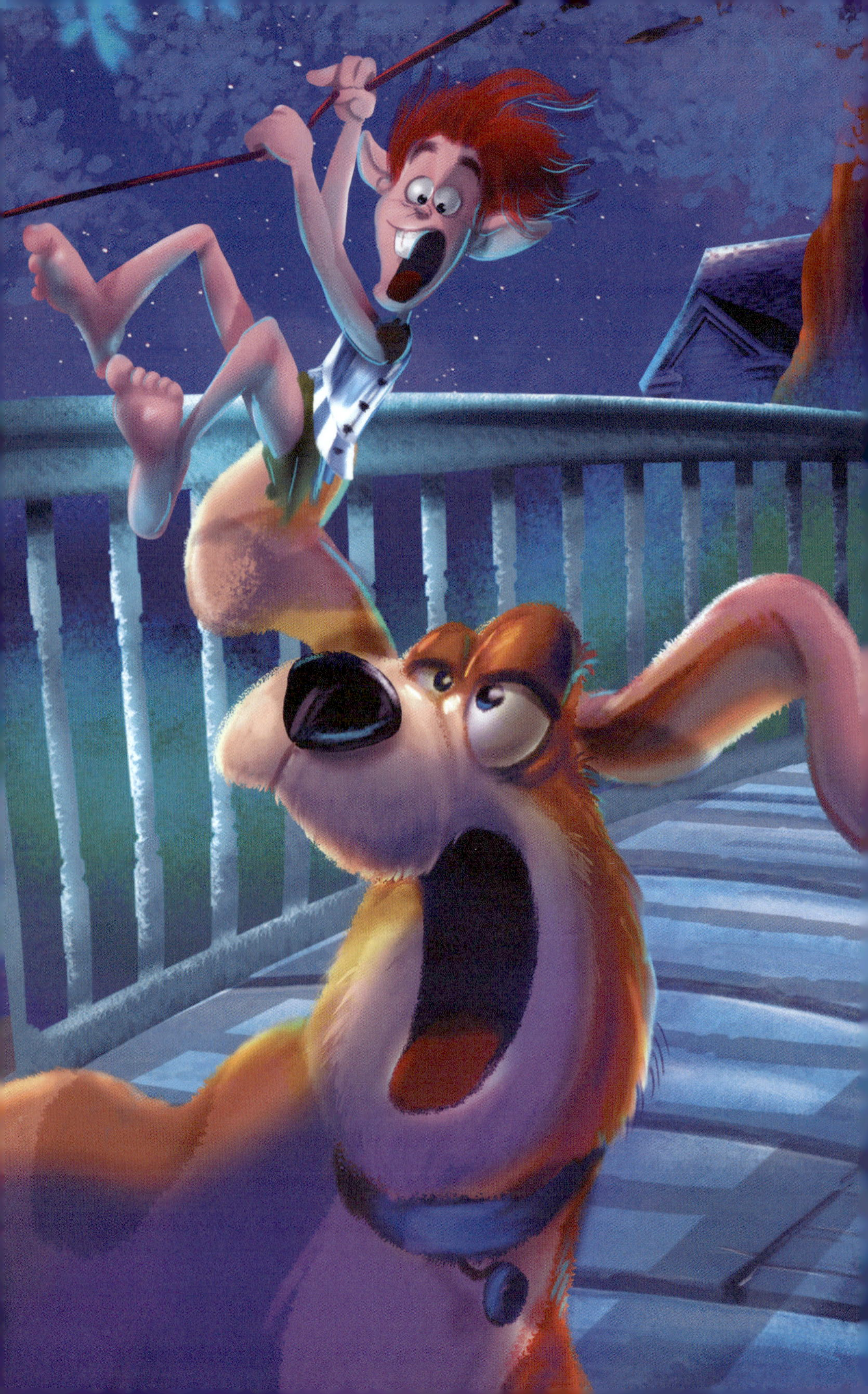

"You okay there, buddy?" said the man.

The dog stopped licking his wounds, got up, wagged his tail at the sight of his master, and walked towards him.

"What are you doing out here?" asked the man, as he bent down to pet him. He held out his hand, The Hound licked it, then pointed his nose at the tree, growling.

"What is it?" said the man, looking up to see the branches swaying.

Boid daren't breathe, as he watched the human peer at them through rounded glasses and squinted his eyes. The man looked up at The Moon for a moment, then down to The Hound.

"Let's get you inside," he said, "The full moon always drives you crazy."

The man headed towards the door, and The Hound followed, seemingly glancing back at them in annoyance.

Boid gazed up, to see Fluff being heaved over the edge of the gutter and out of sight, by a determined mini marvel, Luna. When he looked back down, the human and dog had stepped back inside. The door clicked shut, and Boid allowed himself a breath. Looking up at The Boy's window, he realised that there wasn't that much of a gap in the opening. It was a classic nooks and crannies situation. He knew, from here, the cadets were on their own.

"It's up to them now," Boid said.

"You think they're up to it?" Jipp asked.

"They'll be fine. It's just a sock. How hard can that be?" Boid reasoned.

Jipp put on a fake smile, and said, "It is a very important sock, though."

Boid knew he was mocking him.

"How will they know which sock is the important one?"

Knowing that Jipp already knew it didn't matter which sock it was, he decided not to rise to the bait of his friend's playful teasing. His mind was elsewhere, on the roof.

The success of the mission now rested on Little Firecracker and Fluff.

CHAPTER EIGHT:
EIGHT LEGS ARE BETTER THAN ANY OTHER NUMBER

As she lay breathless in the gutter, Luna looked at Fluff and said, "You okay?"

"His breath was so funky, I can still smell it," panted Fluff, "It's horrible!"

"I think you passed directly through his jaws! It was incredible!"

"Yeah," Fluff replied, "Incredibly horrible."

Luna let out a little giggle, and climbed to her feet. Fluff stood up, and they both shared a moment of relief. Luna's next thought was to check the condition of the wire, which was stretched and scraped by the gutter edge, looking worn.

Would it be safe for two more wire climbs, and could I hurl it back across?

She looked up at The Boy's window above them, and saw it was open by the smallest of gaps. Boid would struggle to squeeze his barrel chest through, and by the time they had reattached the wire to get them across, they could have been in there and sock hunting. So, she weighed up the risks, considered time was of the essence, and decided it was up to them.

"It's up to us," she said.

Fluff's bucked teeth nipped at his bottom lip, and he said, "Where do you get all that confidence from?"

"It's too risky for them to use the wire again, the wire's too damaged to take their weight," she said, pointing to worn wire, "It would probably be just about good enough to take our weight on the climb down, but not in a fit state to be used for two bigger Beams. Besides, we're the only ones small enough for incursion," and she pointed to the window.

"Incursion?" remarked Fluff, looking at her, "When did you swallow a military dictionary?"

Luna smiled at him with the smile she always used, to get her own way.

"It is just a sock, Luna," Fluff quibbled.

"Yes," Luna mockingly responded, "But it's a sock of great importance."

"That's exactly what Commander Boid said," Fluff replied.

Luna knew he had been hoping they would get to play poltergeist for the night, and if she were honest, she had hoped the same. But she was riding a wave after her miraculous resurrection, and decided to put a positive spin on it.

"Come on, this is what it's all about. We wanted adventure, didn't we?" she said, "Think of it as a story waiting to be told."

"A story about a sock," Fluff replied, "No one tells stories about socks."

"It could be a story about the journey towards the sock," Luna suggested, "All you need to do is tell it with charm. A good story is what you make it."

Fluff looked up, and pondered for a moment. Luna maintained the smile.

"Okay, you win," he conceded, "Although, I've absolutely no idea how I'm going to be able to dream up a thrilling story about sock-theft."

It had always been Luna's theory that smiling got you a long way, and she liked to prove it on a regular basis. In her view, smiling was infectious, and if you smile, others were more likely to smile with you. And when they're smiling, they're more likely to agree with your point of view.

With her friend on board, she jumped up to the gutter edge, grabbed it, and peered over to signal to their commander. He and Jipp were crouched on the branch, patiently waiting. She waved, he waved back, and that was good enough for her. She was certain Boid had already done the same calculations, and reached the same conclusion. The conclusion that it was up to her and her pal. They were going to get that sock, and they were going to be blooming magnificent doing it.

She let go of the edge, dropped, turned to Fluff, and said, "Let's go sock-hunting."

They both made the jump up from the gutter, onto the sloped roof, and scrambled up the tiles, as silently as they could. They climbed up onto the window cill, and looked inside.

The room was only lit by borrowed passages of light from the outside, but she could make out its dimensions, and the

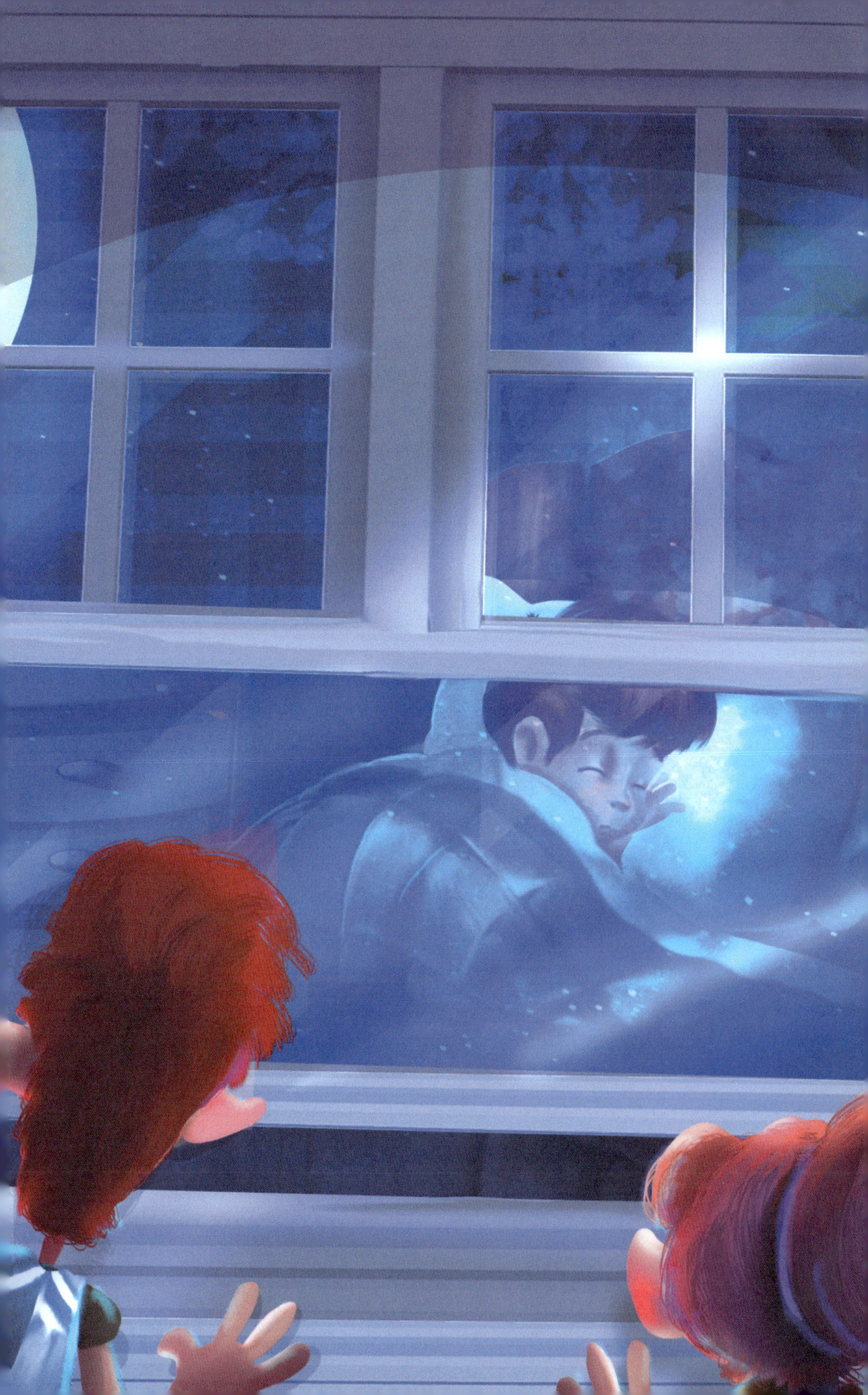

positions of the furniture. The Boy lay sleeping in his bed, facing the window, with eyes tightly shut. He looked about six or seven years old. Beyond him and the bed, were a set of drawers, with the top drawer left hanging slightly open.

Humans are asking to be pranked, if they leave things open, she thought.

She recognised the open drawer as their best bet, and there was a good chance that residing within that drawer, was a sock or two. Fluff had taken position beside her, laid belly down, and was peering inside too. Then they looked to each other.

"Do you see the open drawer?" Luna whispered.

Fluff gave a silent nod, Luna signalled to move, and they shuffled themselves across the flatness of the cill, to make their incursion. As they squeezed inside, they could see there was a large wooden toy chest just a few inches below the window. When they saw it, they dropped down onto it, and huddled together.

Luna scanned the room again, and noticed the following; The Boy hadn't moved, and looked soundly asleep; The bedroom door, this time, was shut, meaning less chance of dogs; It was only a short distance across the bedroom floor to get to the sock drawer; And there was a baseball glove on the floor beside the toy box. They could use it to break their fall from the box.

Luna turned to Fluff and whispered, "Onto the glove, follow me."

She stood up, walked to the edge of the box, and jumped. When she landed, it wasn't as soft as she expected, but she immediately sprung back up to her feet, as if it was nothing. Fluff took the leap, landed with a dull thud, then clambered to his feet as gracefully as he could. Luna wagged her finger twice, toward the drawers, signalling the move, and they started a sneaky Moonbeam tip-toe across the bedroom floor.

It was deathly silent, and Luna felt like their creeping was top class. It was the sort of single-file silent creeping you could be proud of and, before long they were halfway across the room. Luna was glancing over at The Boy to see he remained undisturbed, when she heard a noise. She stopped still, and Fluff had to do the same, so he didn't walk into the back of her.

"You hear that?" she whispered.

Fluff pricked up his ears and hushed, "Hear what?"

"Not sure," Luna replied, "Sounded a bit like really sarcastic laughter."

"I don't hear anything," Fluff said.

Luna's eyes darted around the room, glaring into the darkest corners, but there was nothing.

"Must've been the radio they have on, downstairs," Luna reasoned.

"Come on, we're nearly there," Fluff urged, nodding his head at the dresser.

Luna looked at his face for a moment, decided he was right, then resumed creeping.

"Har, Har, Har," came a faint voice from the night.

Luna focused her gaze in the direction of the voice, and saw something coming towards them across the bedroom floor. From the shadows of the room corner, scuttled two round-bellied house spiders, with eyes like black soap-sud bubbles. They looked like they had something to say, and were followed by dozens of baby spiders, forming an orderly line behind them.

"Har, Har, Har," they guffawed once more, sounding louder, and more sarcastic.

Luna, inspired and emboldened, whispered over to them, "Could you please keep the noise down? We're kinda in the middle of something here."

The two spiders ceased scuttling, gave each other a bubble-eyed look, and muttered between themselves for a few moments.

Then came a mocking voice from the left spider,

"Two legs!"

Luna looked to Fluff, and then back at them.

"Two legs?" she quizzed.

"Yeah, you only have two legs. Har, Har," said the spider.

"So, what?" Luna asked.

"We've got eight legs," said the spider on the right.

"What's your point?" enquired Luna.

The spiders looked at each other, muttered between themselves again, but did not answer.

"Well, it's been nice talking to you, but we have a mission to complete," Luna said, turning away dismissively.

She looked up at the dresser, trying to decide how to get up there, and she figured by using the drawer handles to climb up, they could do it. They trotted on, left the spiders in their weird conference, and took position at the side of the dresser.

"Fluff," Luna called, "Remember when we were talking about nicknames, and I couldn't think of one for you? Well, I've thought of one."

"What is it?" Fluff enquired.

"You have to earn it," she replied, cryptically.

Fluff stiffened, a puzzled a look in his eye.

"That top drawer is open, and I bet there's a sock in there," she said, "If you can scale the dresser, fish out a sock, and launch it at me, you will have earned the name Tree-Frog Fluff."

"Tree-Frog Fluff?" he squeaked, mockingly. His eyebrows went big, and his hair seemed to bristle.

"Yes," she replied, "Have you ever heard the term 'nimble like a tree-frog'? Well, that's what you are; A nimble tree-frog," she tried to sell it.

"Tree-Frog Fluff?" he remarked, "It hardly rolls off the tongue, does it? I think it needs a bit more work."

Luna smiled, and had to agree. She had thought of others, but thought it would be fun to see how he would react to this one, and to see if he could actually say it.

"I'll tell you what," Fluff said, "I'll tree-frog right up there, spit a sock right at your noodle, and when we turn the bad boy over to The Man, I want you to have thought up a much better nickname than that."

Luna let out a light giggle,

"You're on. I got plenty others to chose from," she teased,

"You go, I'll keep an eye on these guys," she pointed her eyes in the direction of the spiders.

Fluff was straight on it. He jumped to grab the lowest

drawer handle, and began his climb upwards. Luna watched him at first but heard sarcastic laughter again, so she turned around. That's when she noticed the spiders were coming towards her again.

"Admit it. Eight legs are better than two," said the spider on the left.

"I beg your pardon?" replied Luna, confused.

"Eight legs are better than two, I want you to admit it," the spider replied.

"And why would I do that?"

"Because if you don't, my boys over there will crawl all over our roommate's face, and wake him up," threatened the spider, pointing a spindly leg at The Boy.

This revealed their affectionate name for The Boy, but also their lack of affection for Moonbeams. When she looked, the baby spiders were indeed heading towards The Boy, in a line on the floor and knew, that if they woke him up, the mission would be a failure.

"And why would you be so mean?" asked Luna, annoyed.

"Har, har, har!" was the sarcastic sounding response.

Man, it's difficult getting sense out of spiders, she thought.

However, the mission could be compromised, so she decided to do as they asked.

"Ok, I admit it. Eight legs are better than two," she conceded.

"Har, har, har," came the spiders' laugh again.

The laughter finished abruptly, and the spiders started to talk between themselves once more. The one on the left seemed to be gloating, as if he had just won some kind of bet. Then, without warning, they shuffled off silently, back in the direction of the dark corner they came from, using all of the legs they had. When they saw this, the baby spider line changed direction, and started to follow them.

Spiders are weird, thought Luna.

Looking up, she could see Fluff's two legs already dangling out of the top drawer, as he groped around to find the sock. Then, they disappeared, and there was silence for a moment. A light

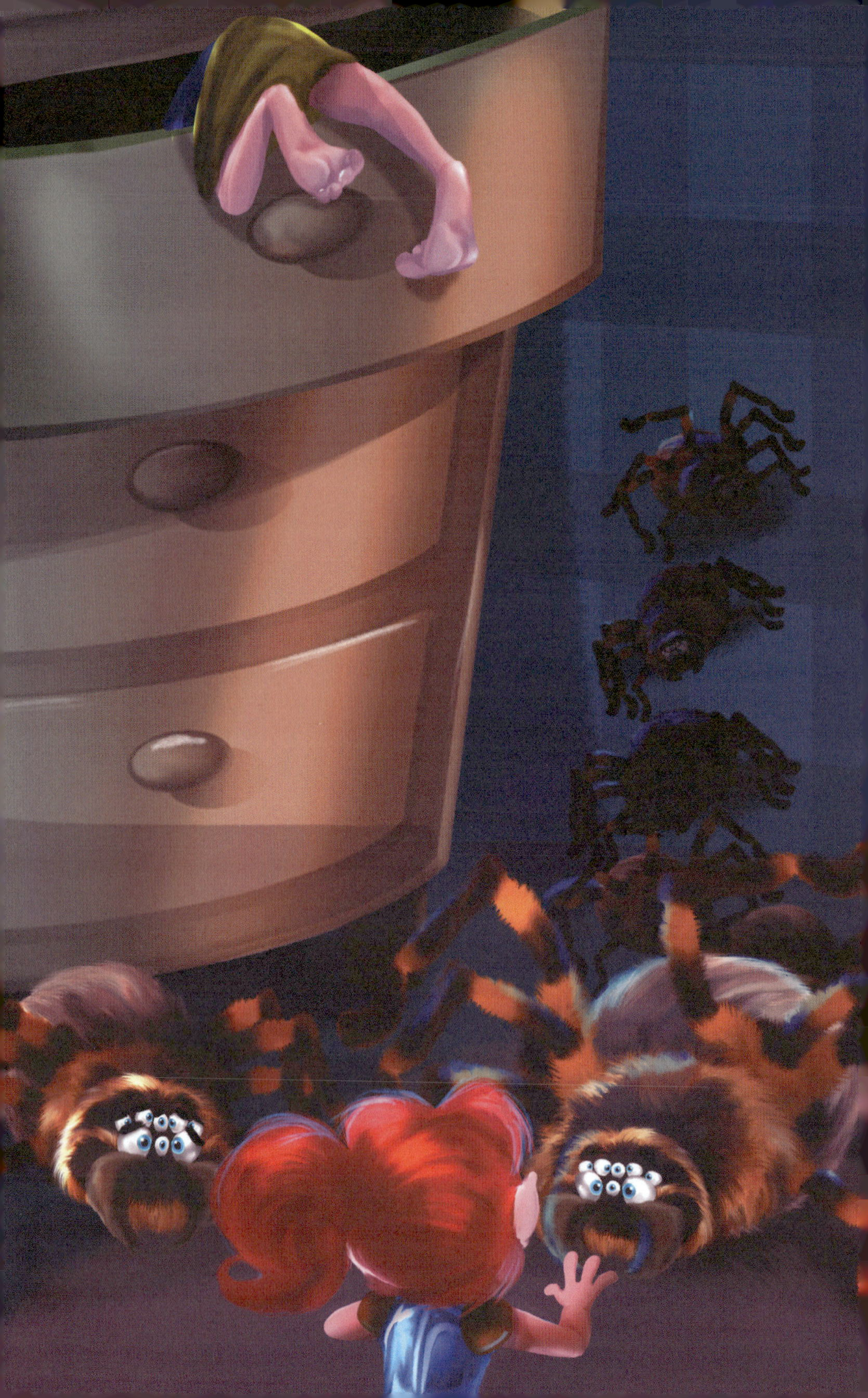

grunt came from inside the drawer, and a sock came hurtling out. It hit the bottom handle, flopped over, and tumbled to Luna's feet. She looked up to see Fluff was peering over the edge of the drawer, silently smiling in victory.

We've got it. It will take us both to carry it out of the room, but we've got it.

Luna looked at the sock, and wondered what was so special about it, then quickly decided now wasn't the time to question it. They needed to get out of there before there were any more interruptions.

Get back quick and take the win, she thought.

Fluff jumped, landed on his feet beside her, and stood proudly over the sock, as if it was some great beast he had defeated in battle.

"Let's get outta here," Luna suggested.

Fluff nodded, and bent down to grab one end of the sock. Luna did the same, and they started tip-toeing back across the room toward the window, carrying the sock between them, like a giant footballer's stretcher. When they reached halfway across, they noticed movement in The Boy's bed. It looked as if he was waking up.

Oh, no! We're so close, Luna thought.

They started to run faster, to get cover behind the toy box. When they reached it, they hid behind it, stopped, and listened. Luna turned to peer around the box to look at The Boy, but all he had done was roll over, and was still fast asleep.

"We're good," Luna whispered.

When she turned back to Fluff, he had already figured out how to get the sock up onto the box, and was rolling it up into a ball. When he finished, he looked up.

"Here, help me throw this up," he whispered, pointing to the top of the box.

She took the balled-up sock on one side while Fluff took the other side, and they started to swing it back and forth.

"On three," Fluff whispered, "One…two…three,"

On three, they let go, launching the sock skywards.

Surprisingly, it landed on the box lid, first time. They looked at each other and smiled, in joint-congratulation. Then, without words, Fluff jumped up and grabbed a metal handle halfway up the side of the toy chest. He lifted up his feet, stood up on the handle, and jumped again. He gripped the edge and lifted himself up, rolled his body onto the box lid, and peered over the edge at Luna.

Luna looked up and, with her being shorter, she realised she would have trouble taking the same leap. Before she could figure out what to do, the unravelled sock flopped down by the side of her head.

Holding one end tightly with his long arms over the edge, Fluff whispered,

"Grab it, I'll pull you up."

Luna took hold of the sock, and Fluff started to heave. Then he stood up, walked backwards, and slowly pulled her to the top. When she got there, she clambered over the edge, got to her feet, and looked proudly at Fluff.

What a great team we make, she thought.

They took a second to catch their breath, then looked through the open window, to see Boid frantically beckoning them to hurry. They took one last look back at The Boy, saw that he still looked asleep, and made their way to the window. Fluff climbed out first, and Luna pushed the sock over the cill and through the gap, so he could grab it. When she had squeezed out herself, she saw Boid smiling.

He looks impressed, she thought.

Boid then started signalling to the ground. He was instructing them to get down to the front garden, where he would meet them. Then he and Jipp started to make their way back down the tree. Luna could see the spider wire was still attached to the window roof, draped down the front of the house, and onto the balcony below.

She took the sock-ball and gave it a triumphant kick. It rolled down the roof, flew off the edge, hit the balcony handrail, and bounced onto the garden below. Then, without hesitation Luna grabbed the line, and started to abseil down. When she got to the balcony deck, Fluff then followed her. From the deck, they shimmied down the corner post, and bounced across the lawn to meet Boid and Jipp.

"Well done, cadets," Boid said, "That was truly impressive,"

When they reached him, he gave both of them a firm, proud pat on the back. Luna took the praise warmly, beaming with pride at their achievement. She paused a moment, and realised her mysterious saviour Moonbeam was nowhere to be seen.

Where did she go? she thought.

Why hadn't she stuck around to see her moment of glory?

Somehow, she had felt the need to impress her, and felt cheated by her absence, but Boid's praise was enough for now, and she had plenty of stories to tell her Academy classmates. The mission had been a success, and they had got what they came for. She was still no wiser as the reason, but it was definitely a sock-theft story worth telling. And being in the team that brought about peace with the crabs could even help earn her a place in Moonbeam history.

Would I get some sort of recognition? Luna thought, *Boid seems happy, maybe he'll be rewarded, and then he'll reward me?*

Luna's story would be about the journey; the bright lights of the bustling city, a narrow escape from being squished by a truck, and almost being eaten by a dog. Not forgetting a rare meeting with The Earthtimer. She was awesome, and a real mysterious force. She wished to meet her again someday, to tell her how much she appreciated not being squished or eaten. Then, of course, it was hard to forget the weird spider encounter. That part of the story, however, she would keep to herself because spiders were annoying.

"We're exposed, let's go home with our prize," Boid announced, ever the Commander.

Jipp grabbed the sock, rolled it up, slung it powerfully over his shoulder, and started walking away from the house. They had achieved their mission it was time to beam home.

When they all reached the road Boid looked up at The Moon, still brightly visible in the night sky. The team took their positions, and lined up beside him.

"Bring on Fiji," Boid muttered to himself.

Luna had no idea what he meant, but she did have a random thought. Turning to Fluff she smiled knowingly.

"I've just thought what your nickname can be," she said.

Fluff looked at her, waiting.

"Spider-Fluff," she said with relish.

"I like it," Fluff replied with a grin, "But I've only got two legs, y'know."

Standing there in the moonlight it only took a few moments for Luna to feel an unfamiliar tingle on her skin. Her molecules started to vibrate with the uncontrollable pull of home. Then, in a flash of light, they were dispatched the same speed, back to The Moon. Luna hoped her story wouldn't end with a face full of Moon dust.

The street was left in silence. It was as if they had never even been there. However, what they hadn't noticed was a young face watching them from the window they had just come from. The Boy had been pretending to be asleep the whole time, and had seen everything.

EPILOGUE: THE FUTURE IS WRITTEN

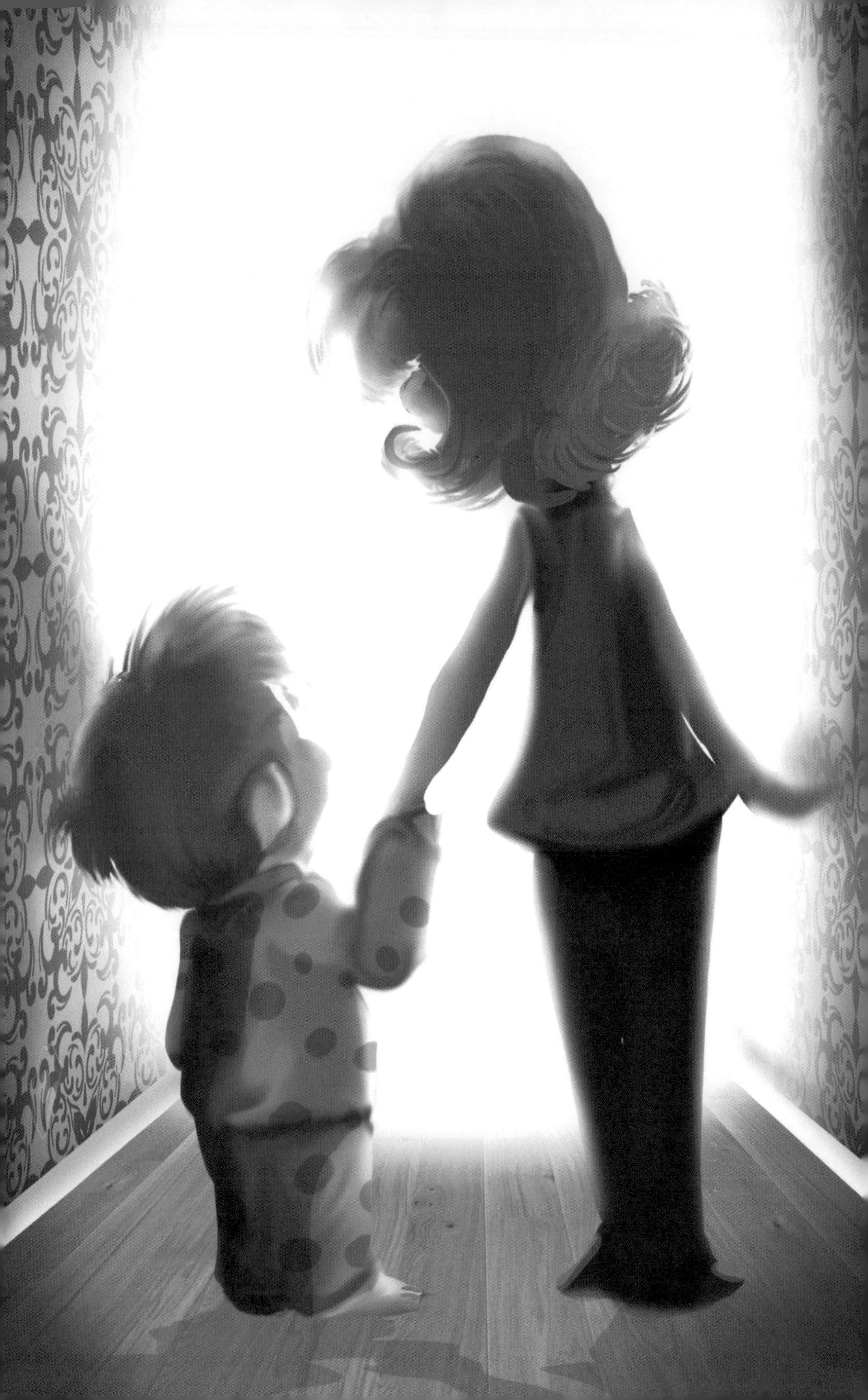

The Boy had stayed up all night thinking about his mysterious little visitors, and in the morning, when he got dressed for school, he was wearing only one sock. He was sat on his toy box, gazing out of the bedroom window, when he heard his mother shouting,

"John! It's time for school!"

But The Boy did not respond. He was too busy trying to figure out what it was he had seen the night before.

What were those tiny elf-like creatures, and why had they stolen one of his socks?

His mother must have been waiting for him to say he was coming, because she called up once again, this time a little more sternly,

"John Fitzgerald Kennedy, get yourself down here, right this instant, or we'll be late."

He noticed the tone of her voice, got up from the box, and made his way downstairs. As he reached the bottom of the stairs, his mother was waiting for him.

She looked him up and down, and said, "Where's your other sock?"

"They took it," he answered.

"Who took it?" she asked.

"The others," he explained, "They took it to The Moon."

His mother looked him in the eye and smiled.

"Oh, John, you have such an active imagination," she replied, "Now let's get going."

His mother locked the front door, ushered him in the direction of the car, and followed on behind him.

It was a bright day, and the sunshine glinted in the windows of the distant completed, and half-completed sky rise buildings of 1920s Boston City.

As John got in the car he said to his mother,

"One day I'll go to The Moon, and get my sock back."

As his mother got in the car she said,

"Sure, honey. Anything's possible."

THE END

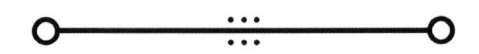

'We choose to go to The Moon. We choose to go to The Moon in this decade and do the other things, not because they are easy, but because they are hard, because that goal will serve to organise and measure the best of our energies and skills, because that challenge is one that we are willing to accept, one we are unwilling to postpone, and one which we intend to win, and the others, too.'

> - John Fitzgerald Kennedy
>   35th President of The United States
>   Rice Stadium Moon Speech
>   September 12th, 1962

Was this the same boy,
the same John Fitzgerald Kennedy?
What did he mean by 'and the others, too'?
Was he talking about The Moonbeams?

DON'T MISS THE NEXT EPISODE:

THE RETURN OF THE EARTHTIMER

The Man has always been the one to pull the strings.
He's the one behind everything.

Every mystery, every secret, and every human advancement. This time he needs to get the team back together for another mission.

A mission of even greater importance.

One he's been planning for a very long time.

A plan to bring The Earthtimer home.

I'd like to thank the following for their inspiration, patience, support, and help in keeping me sane, whilst I told my ridiculously silly story;

My daughter Lana, my wife Sarah, my brothers Steve and Mike, The Willgoose Family, Heather McCaig, Antony & Kristy Smith, Ian Collins, Steve Chapman, Paul Askwith, Paul Bradshaw, Lor Bingham (my fantastic editor) Eduardo,
Andy and Richie at Bear With Us Productions,

Printed in Great Britain
by Amazon

36837527R00050